LEGO

NINJAGO

Masters of Spinjitzu

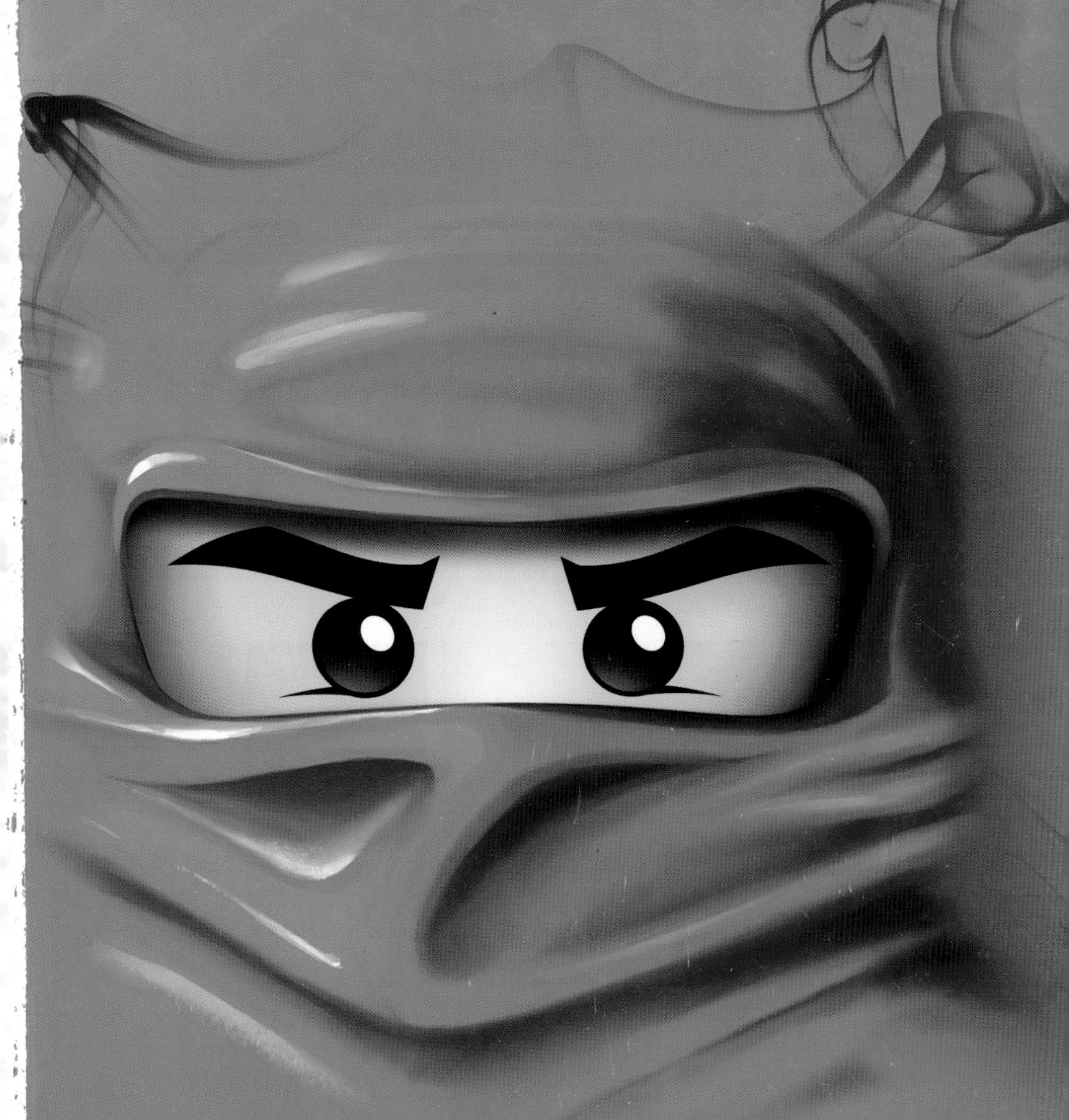

PAPERCUTZ™

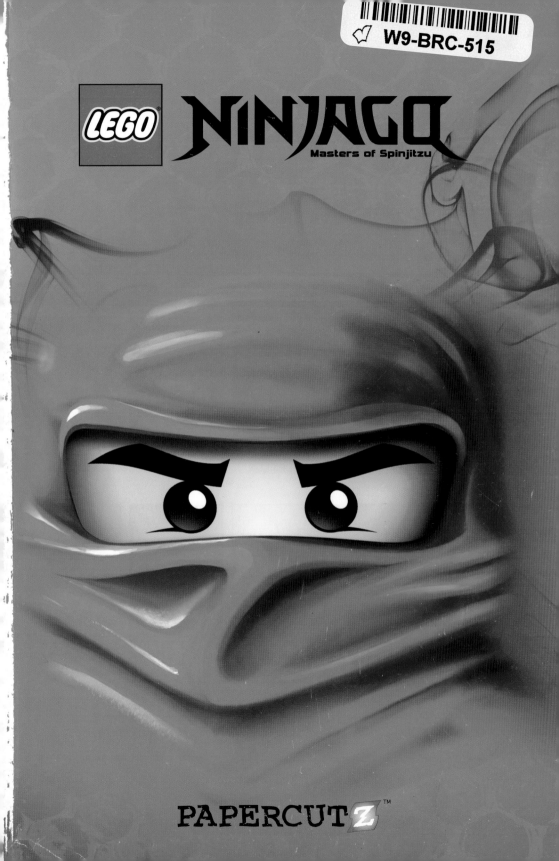

LEGO® GRAPHIC NOVELS AVAILABLE FROM PAPERCUTZ™

ALL-NEW! FULL-COLOR GRAPHIC NOVEL!
LEGO NINJAGO
Masters of Spinjitzu
"THE CHALLENGE OF SAMUKAI!"
GREG FARSHTEY
PAULO HENRIQUE
PAPERCUTZ
NINJAGO #1

ALL-NEW! FULL-COLOR GRAPHIC NOVEL!
LEGO NINJAGO
"MASK OF THE SENSEI"
GREG FARSHTEY
PAULO HENRIQUE
PAPERCUTZ
NINJAGO #2

ALL-NEW! FULL-COLOR GRAPHIC NOVEL!
LEGO NINJAGO
"RISE OF THE SERPENTINE"
GREG FARSHTEY
PAUL LEE
PAPERCUTZ
NINJAGO #3

FULL-COLOR GRAPHIC NOVEL
BIONICLE
#1: RISE OF THE TOA NUVA
GREG FARSHTEY
CARLOS D'ANDA
RANDY ELLIOTT
HOW IT ALL BEGAN...
PAPERCUTZ
LEGO
BIONICLE #1

FULL-COLOR GRAPHIC NOVEL
BIONICLE
GREG FARSHTEY
RANDY ELLIOTT
PAPERCUTZ
LEGO
BIONICLE #2

FULL-COLOR GRAPHIC NOVEL
BIONICLE
#3: CITY OF LEGENDS
GREG FARSHTEY
RANDY ELLIOTT
PAPERCUTZ
LEGO
BIONICLE #3

FULL-COLOR GRAPHIC NOVEL
BIONICLE
#4: TRIAL BY FIRE
GREG FARSHTEY
RANDY ELLIOTT
PAPERCUTZ
LEGO
BIONICLE #4

FULL-COLOR GRAPHIC NOVEL
BIONICLE
#5: THE BATTLE OF VOYA NUI
GREG FARSHTEY
STUART SAYGER
PAPERCUTZ
LEGO
BIONICLE #5

FEATURING HYDRAXON IN AN ALL-NEW STORY!
FULL-COLOR GRAPHIC NOVEL
BIONICLE
#6: THE UNDERWATER CITY
GREG FARSHTEY
STUART SAYGER
CHRISTIAN ZANIER
PAPERCUTZ
LEGO
BIONICLE #6

FULL-COLOR GRAPHIC NOVEL
BIONICLE
#7: REALM OF FEAR
GREG FARSHTEY
LEIGH GALLAGHER
LEGO
BIONICLE #7

ALL-NEW! ALL-OUT AWESOME ACTION!
FULL-COLOR GRAPHIC NOVEL
BIONICLE
#8: LEGENDS OF BARA MAGNA
GREG FARSHTEY
CHRISTIAN ZANIER
LEGO
BIONICLE #8

FULL-COLOR GRAPHIC NOVEL
BIONICLE
#9: FALL OF ATERO
GREG FARSHTEY
POP MHAN
PAPERCUTZ
LEGO
BIONICLE #9

MAKUTA'S GUIDE TO THE UNIVERSE
BIONICLE
Makuta's Guide to the Universe

MATA NUI'S GUIDE TO BARA MAGNA
BIONICLE
Mata Nui's Guide to Bara Magna

NINJAGO graphic novels, BIONICLE® graphic novels, and guide books are available in paperback and hardcover at booksellers everywhere.

Or order from us: please add $4.00 for postage and handling for first book, add $1.00 for each additional book. NINJAGO #1-3 are $6.99 in paperback, and $13.99 in hardcover. BIONICLE #1-3, 8, and 9 are $8.99 in paperback, $13.99 in hardcover. Guide Books are $9.99 each in paperback only. Please make check payable to NBM Publishing.
Send to: Papercutz, 160 Broadway, Ste. 700, East Wing, New York, NY 10038 • 1-800-886-1223

www.papercutz.com

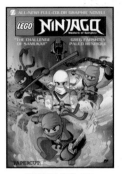

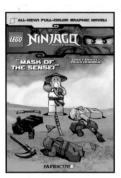

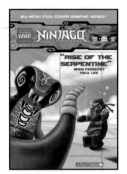

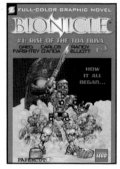

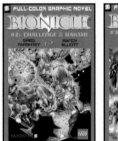

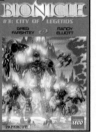

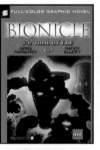

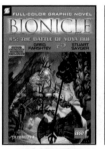

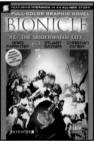

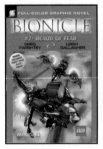

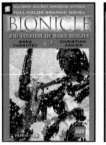

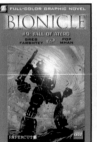

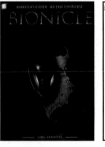

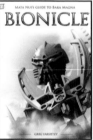

#3 RISE OF THE SERPENTINE

Greg Farshtey • Writer

Paul Lee,
with Space Goat
and Paulo Henrique • Artists

Laurie E. Smith • Colorist

New York

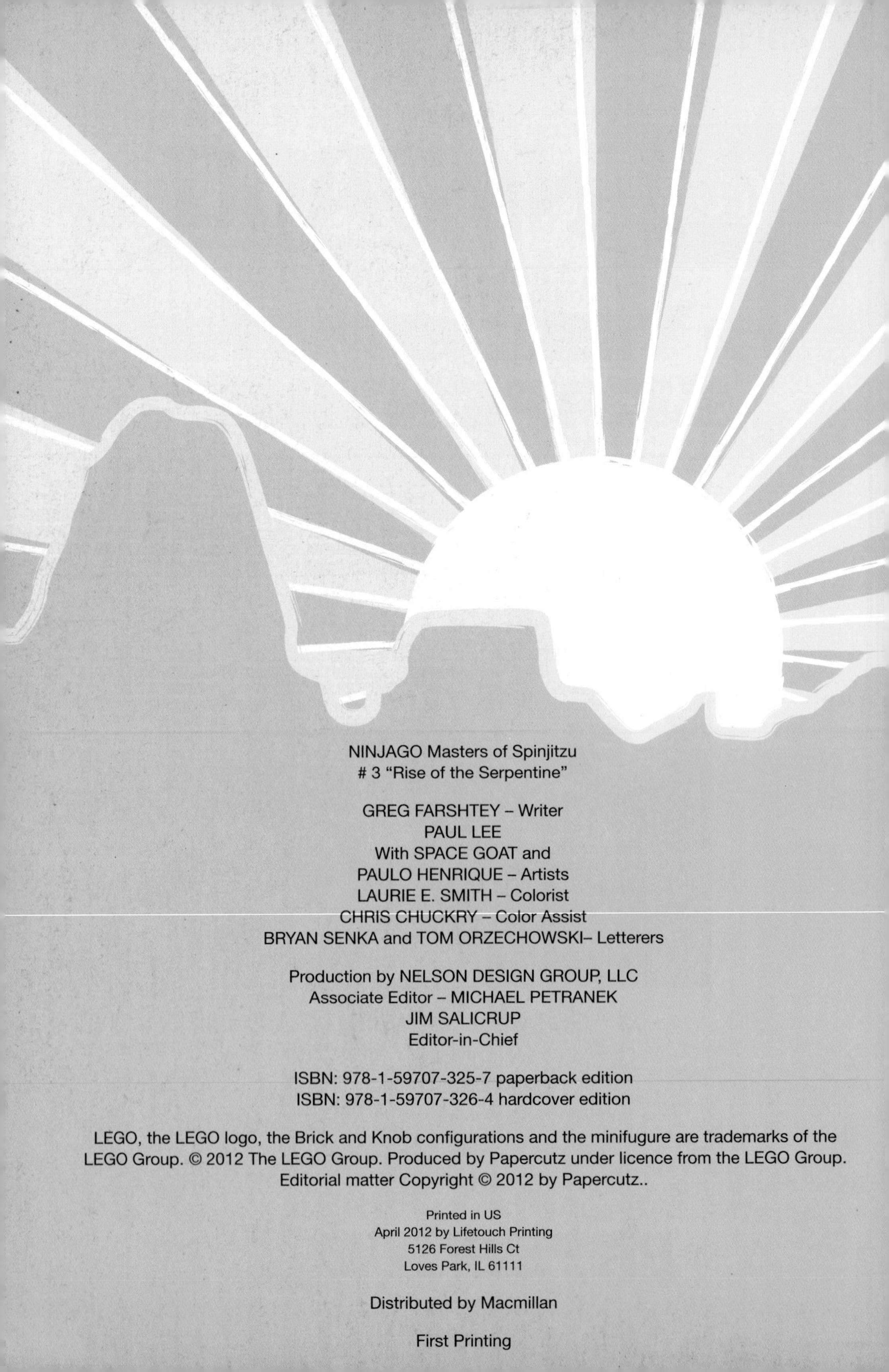

NINJAGO Masters of Spinjitzu
3 "Rise of the Serpentine"

GREG FARSHTEY – Writer
PAUL LEE
With SPACE GOAT and
PAULO HENRIQUE – Artists
LAURIE E. SMITH – Colorist
CHRIS CHUCKRY – Color Assist
BRYAN SENKA and TOM ORZECHOWSKI– Letterers

Production by NELSON DESIGN GROUP, LLC
Associate Editor – MICHAEL PETRANEK
JIM SALICRUP
Editor-in-Chief

ISBN: 978-1-59707-325-7 paperback edition
ISBN: 978-1-59707-326-4 hardcover edition

Printed in US
April 2012 by Lifetouch Printing
5126 Forest Hills Ct
Loves Park, IL 61111

Distributed by Macmillan

First Printing

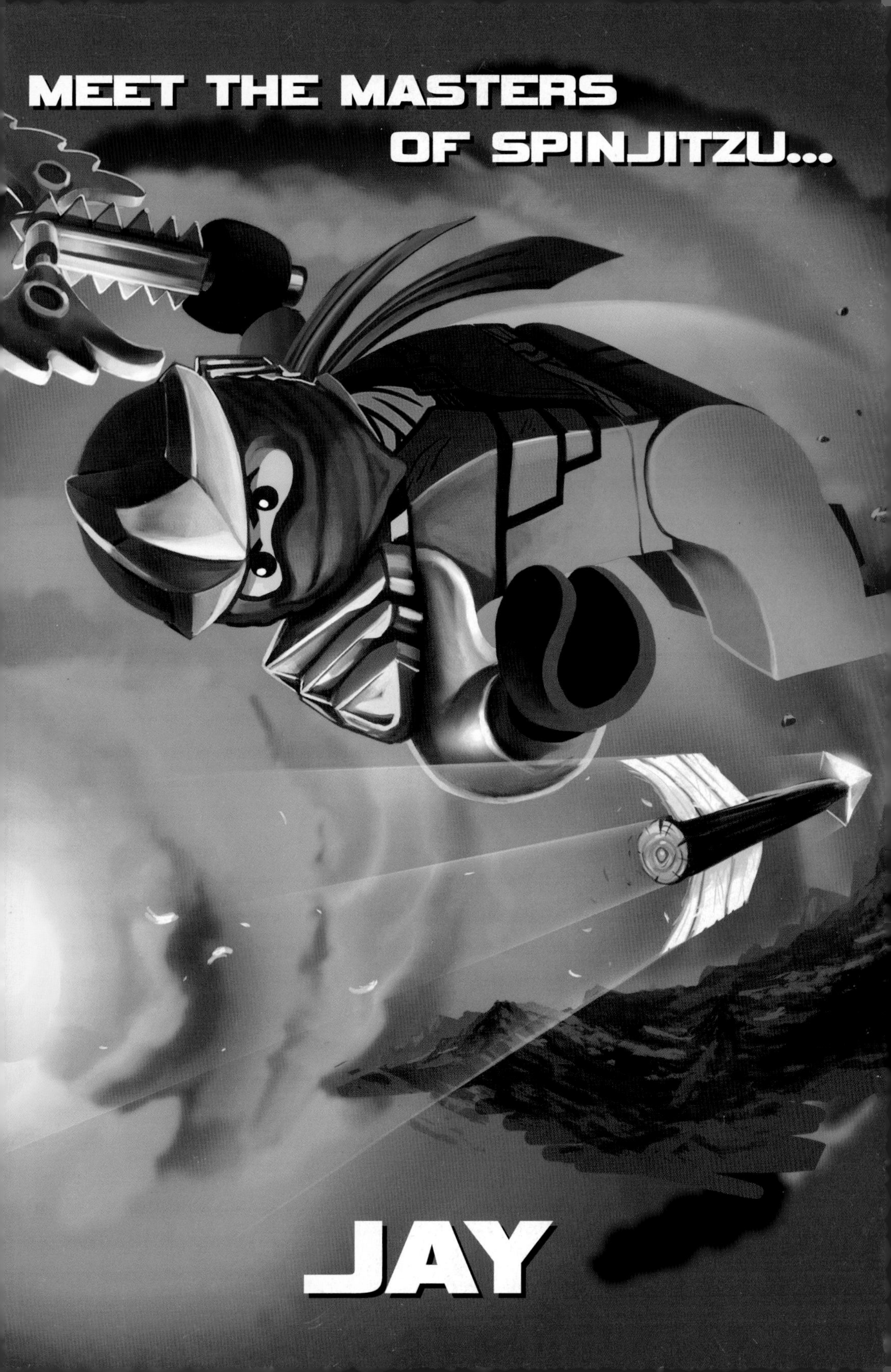
MEET THE MASTERS
OF SPINJITZU...
JAY

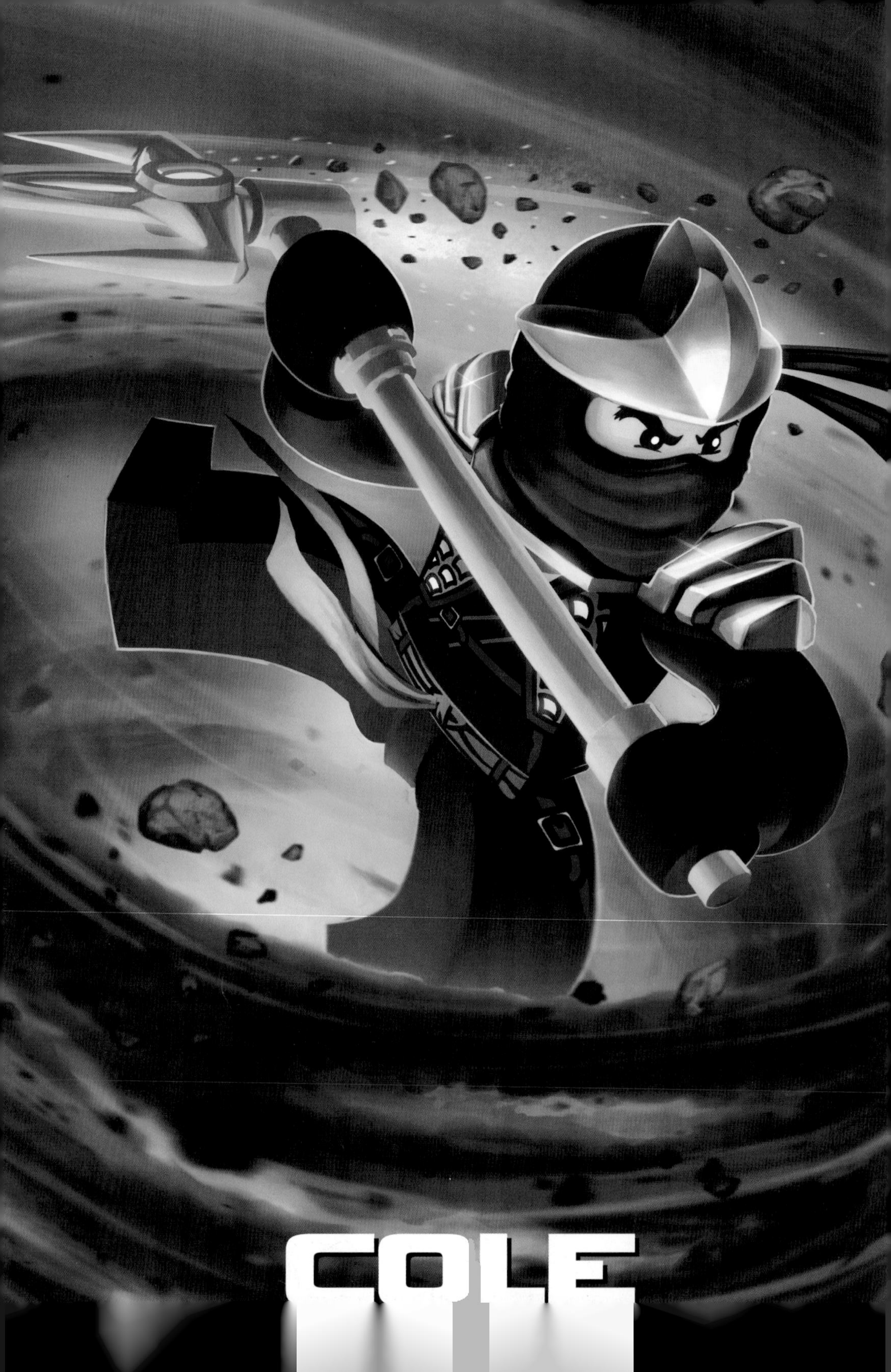
COLE

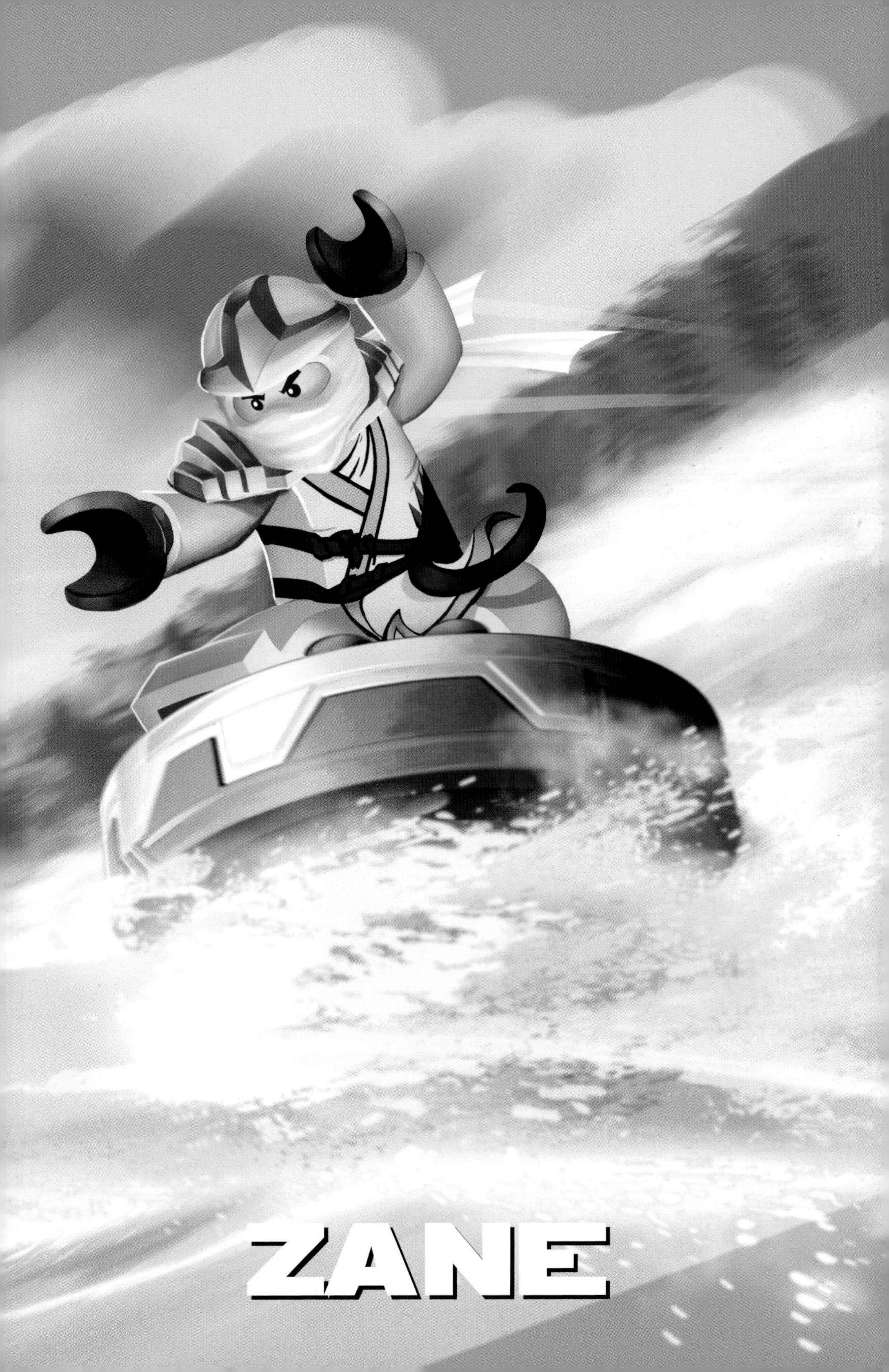
ZANE

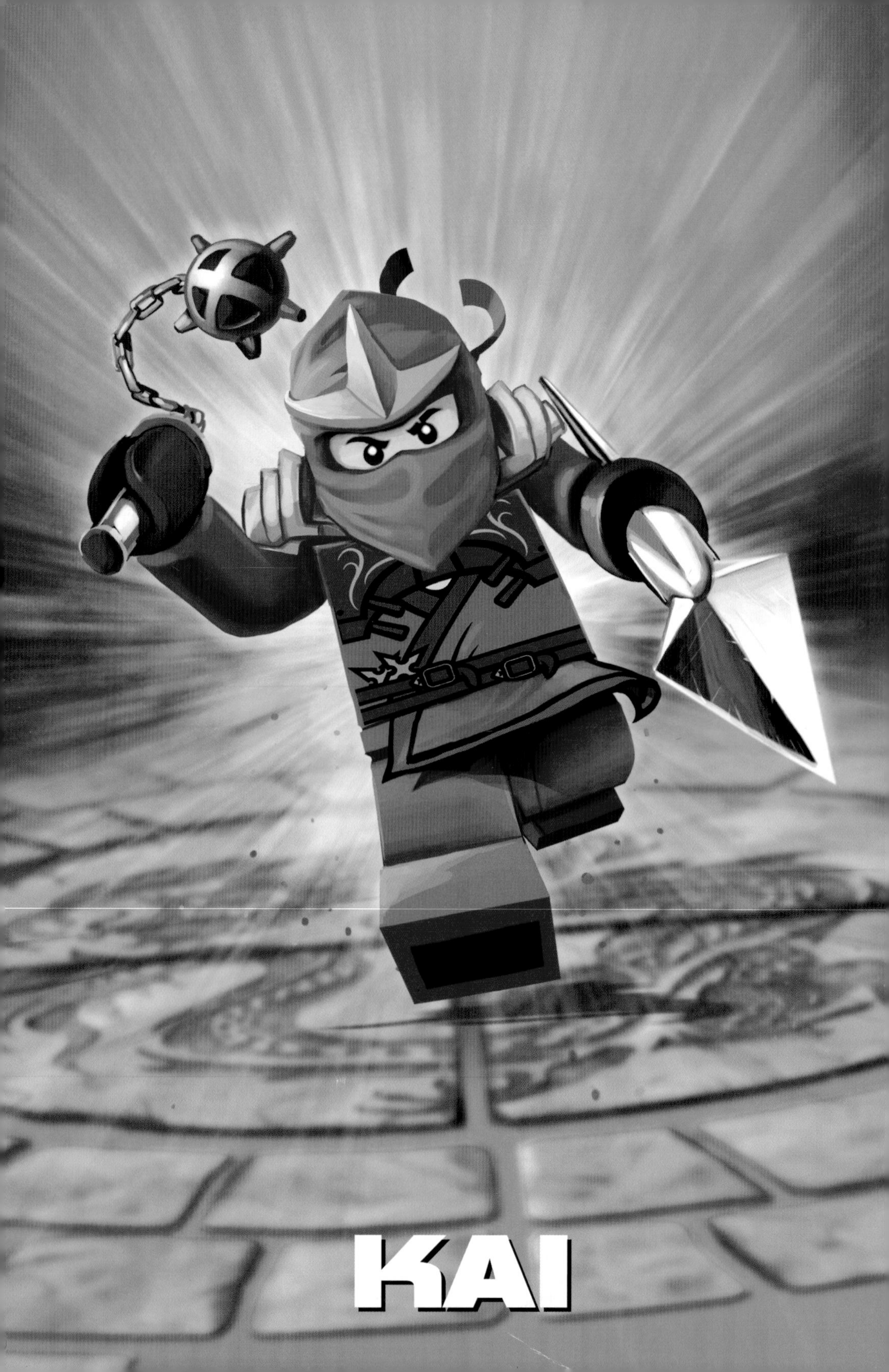
KAI

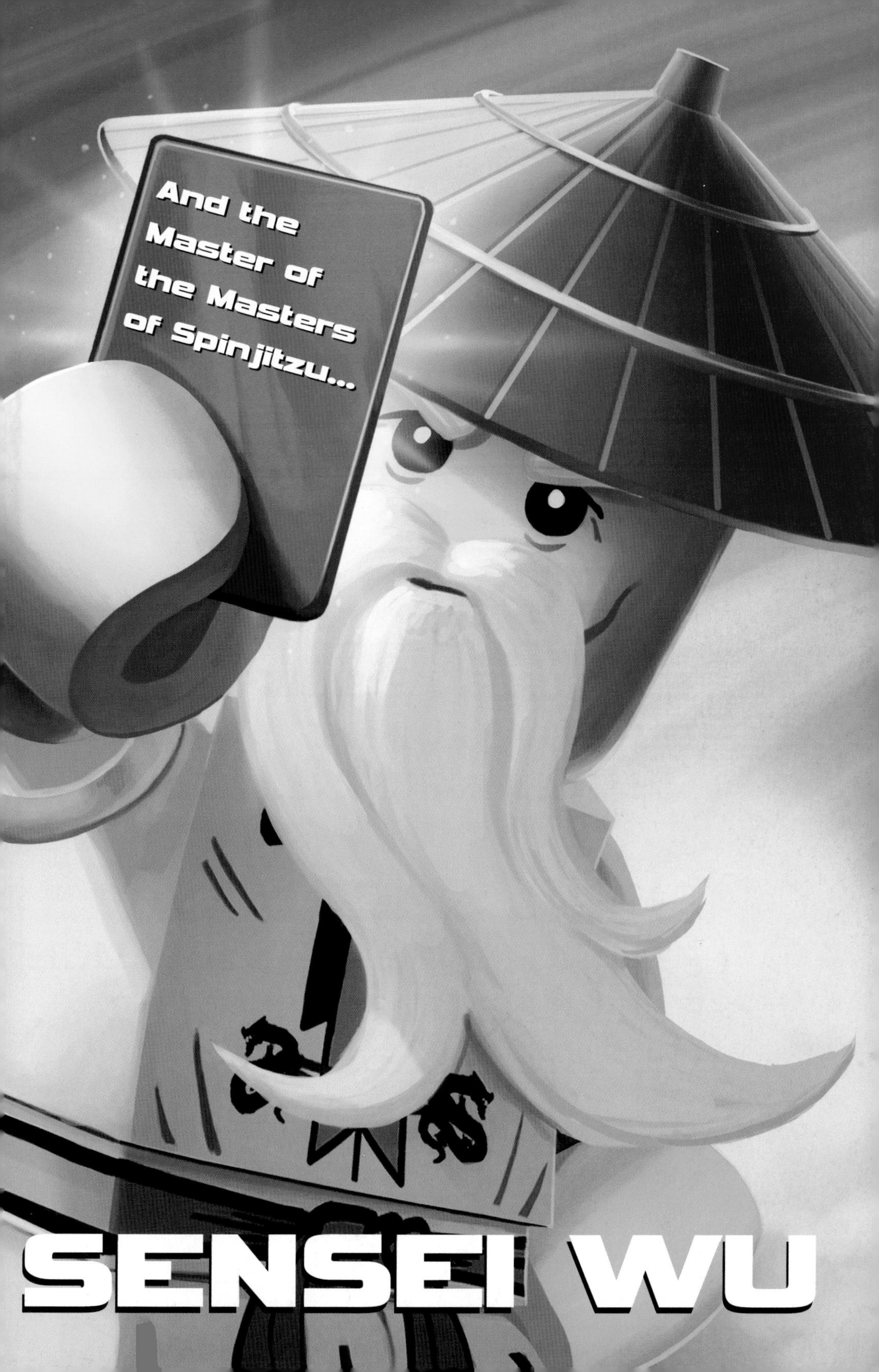
And the Master of the Masters of Spinjitzu...
SENSEI WU

BEWARE!
YOU ARE ABOUT TO ENTER THE WORLD OF NINJAGO . . .

BEWARE!
FOR THE TIME HAS COME FOR THE RISE OF THE SERPENTINE!

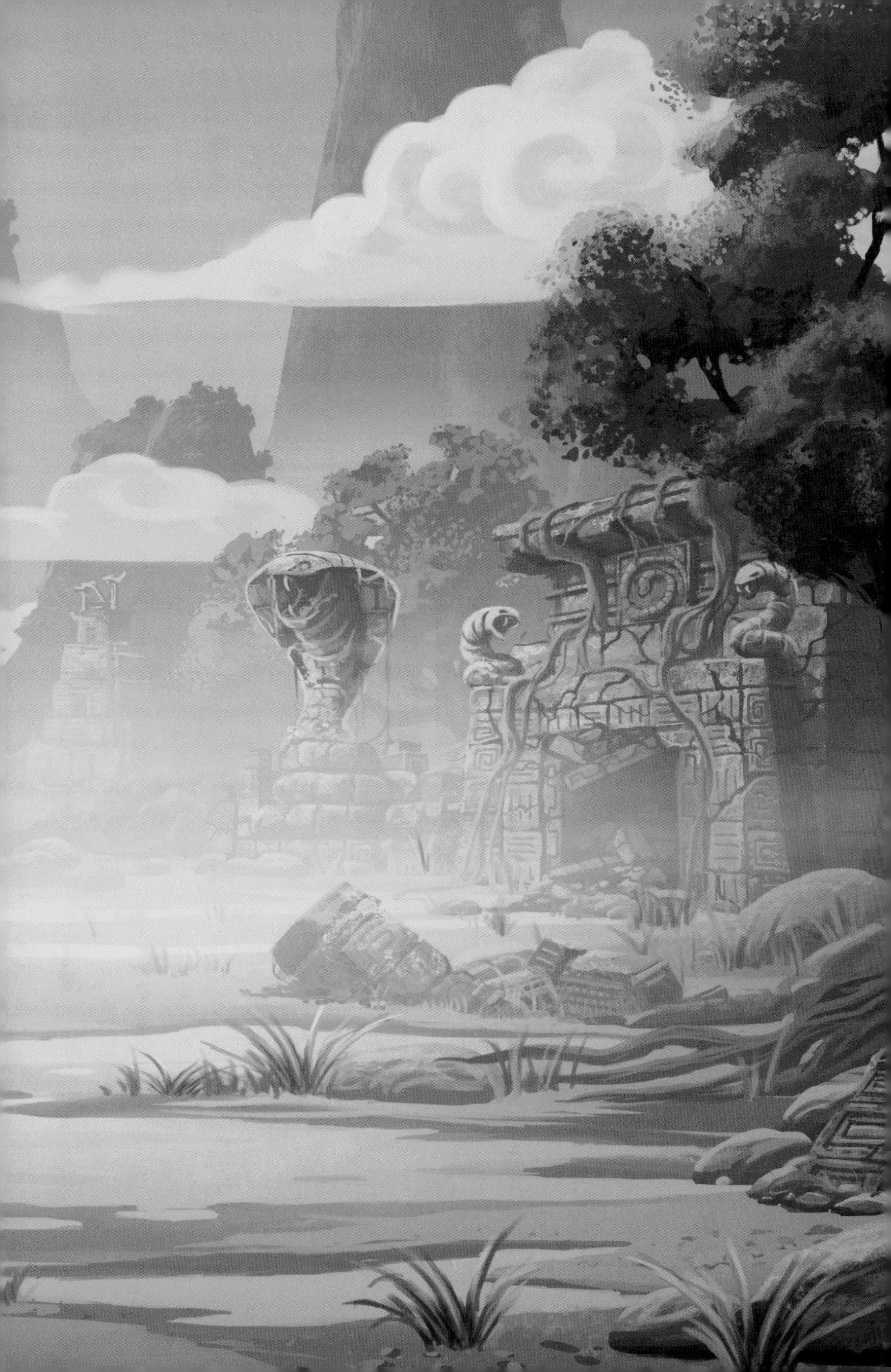

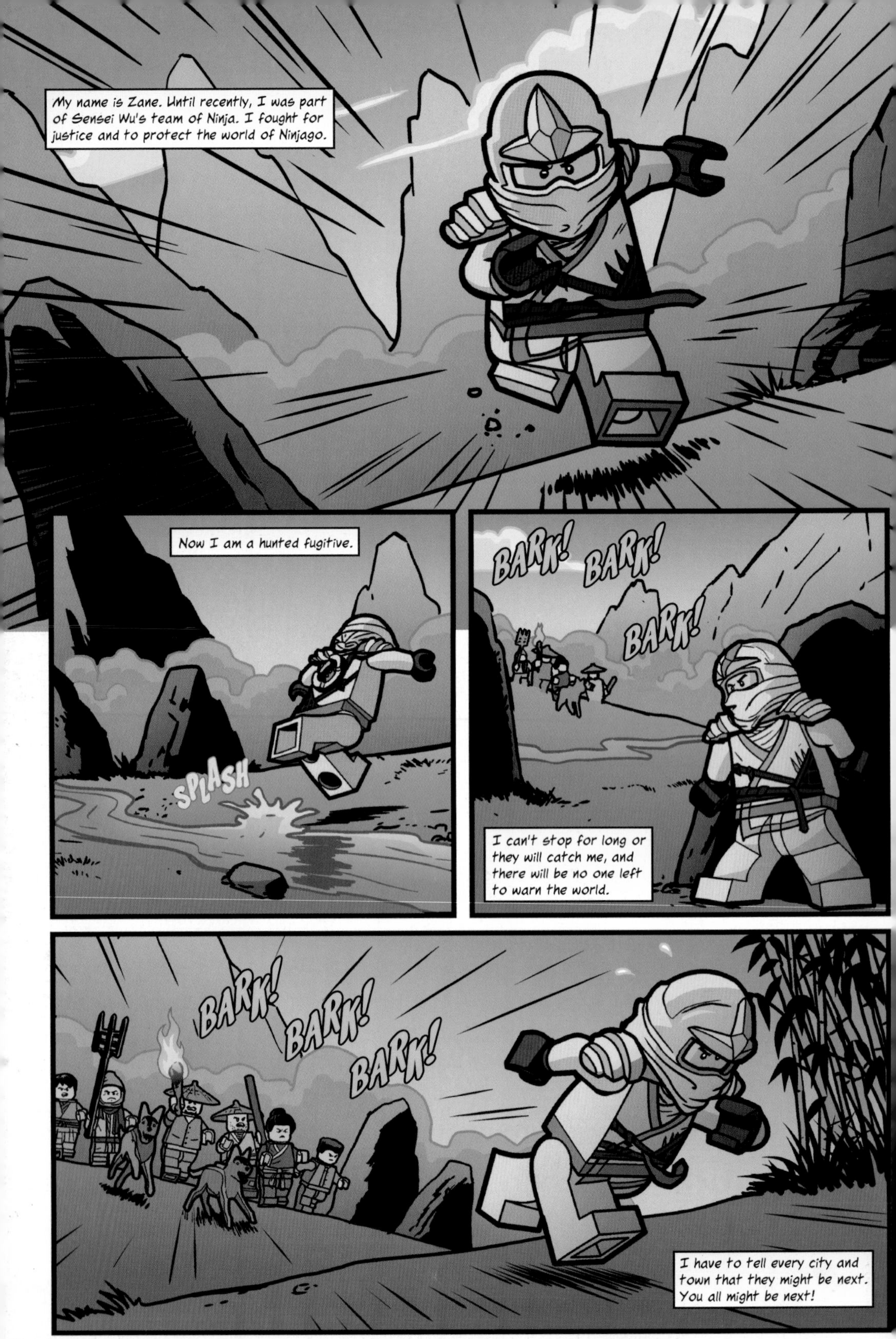
My name is Zane. Until recently, I was part of Sensei Wu's team of Ninja. I fought for justice and to protect the world of Ninjago.
Now I am a hunted fugitive.
SPLASH
BARK! BARK!
BARK!
I can't stop for long or they will catch me, and there will be no one left to warn the world.
BARK!
BARK!
BARK!
I have to tell every city and town that they might be next. You all might be next!

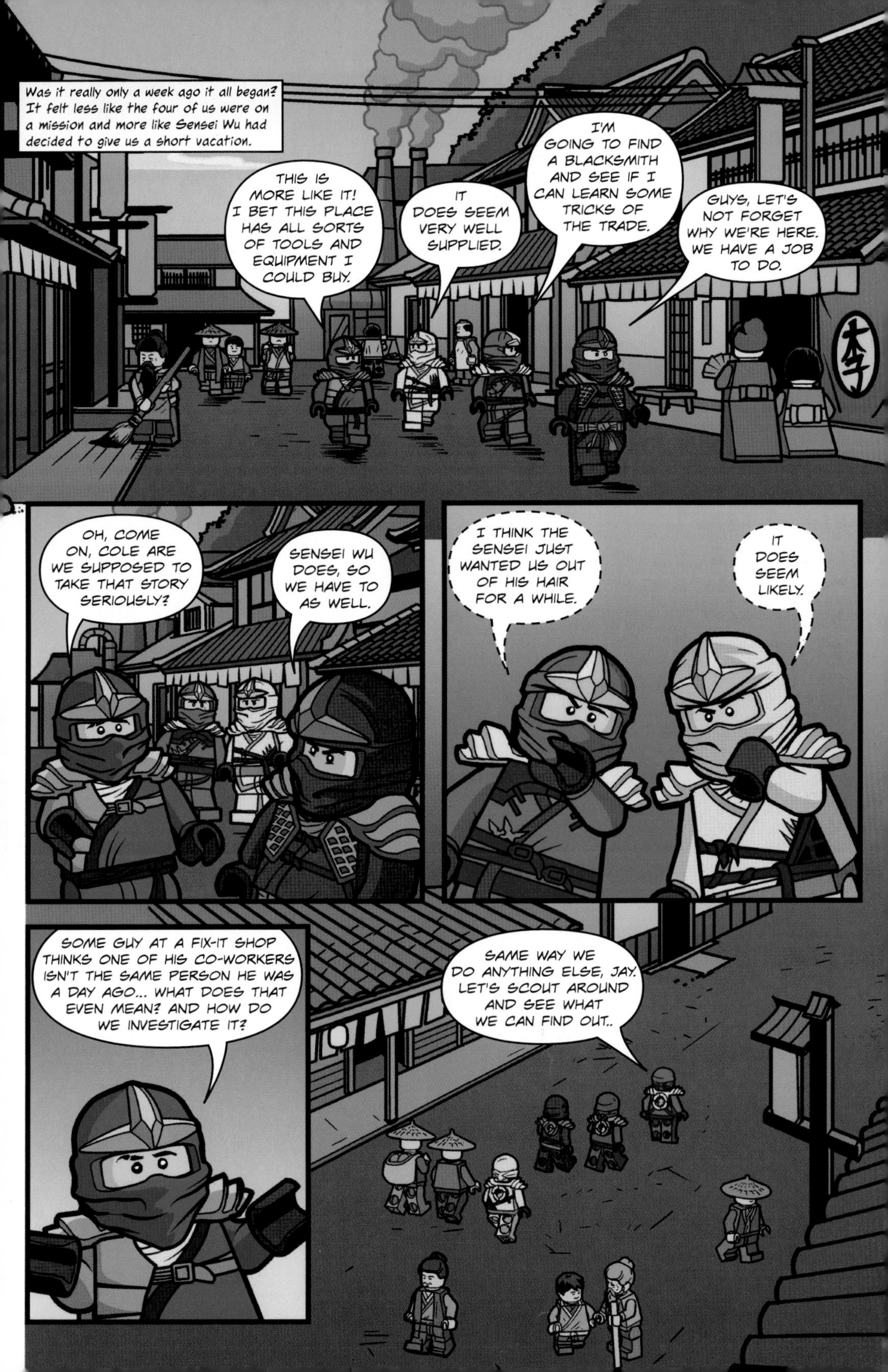
Was it really only a week ago it all began? It felt less like the four of us were on a mission and more like Sensei Wu had decided to give us a short vacation.
THIS IS MORE LIKE IT! I BET THIS PLACE HAS ALL SORTS OF TOOLS AND EQUIPMENT I COULD BUY.
IT DOES SEEM VERY WELL SUPPLIED.
I'M GOING TO FIND A BLACKSMITH AND SEE IF I CAN LEARN SOME TRICKS OF THE TRADE.
GUYS, LET'S NOT FORGET WHY WE'RE HERE. WE HAVE A JOB TO DO.
OH, COME ON, COLE ARE WE SUPPOSED TO TAKE THAT STORY SERIOUSLY?
SENSEI WU DOES, SO WE HAVE TO AS WELL.
I THINK THE SENSEI JUST WANTED US OUT OF HIS HAIR FOR A WHILE.
IT DOES SEEM LIKELY.
SOME GUY AT A FIX-IT SHOP THINKS ONE OF HIS CO-WORKERS ISN'T THE SAME PERSON HE WAS A DAY AGO... WHAT DOES THAT EVEN MEAN? AND HOW DO WE INVESTIGATE IT?
SAME WAY WE DO ANYTHING ELSE, JAY. LET'S SCOUT AROUND AND SEE WHAT WE CAN FIND OUT..

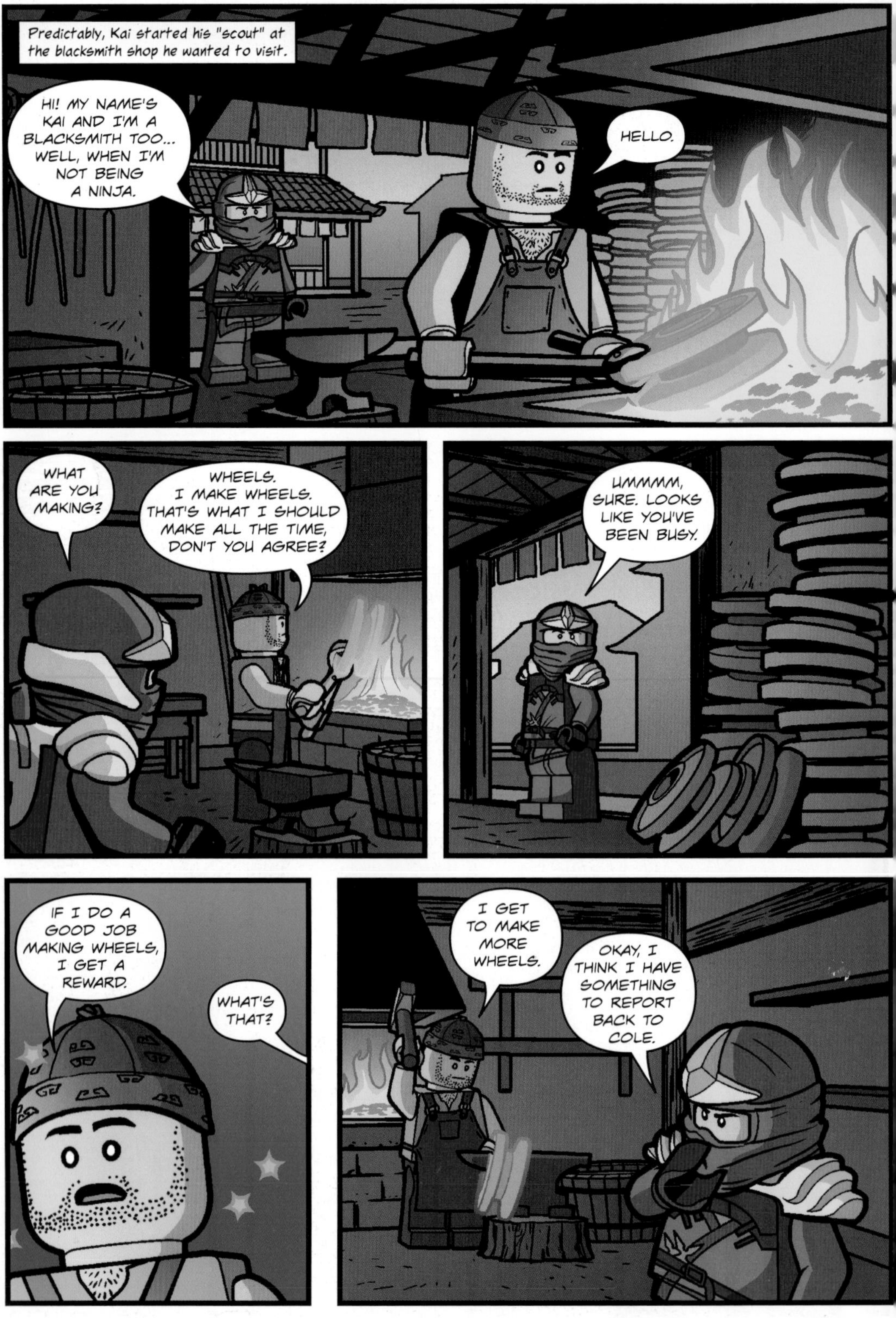
Predictably, Kai started his "scout" at the blacksmith shop he wanted to visit.
HI! MY NAME'S KAI AND I'M A BLACKSMITH TOO... WELL, WHEN I'M NOT BEING A NINJA.
HELLO.
WHAT ARE YOU MAKING?
WHEELS. I MAKE WHEELS. THAT'S WHAT I SHOULD MAKE ALL THE TIME, DON'T YOU AGREE?
UMMMM, SURE. LOOKS LIKE YOU'VE BEEN BUSY.
IF I DO A GOOD JOB MAKING WHEELS, I GET A REWARD.
WHAT'S THAT?
I GET TO MAKE MORE WHEELS.
OKAY, I THINK I HAVE SOMETHING TO REPORT BACK TO COLE.

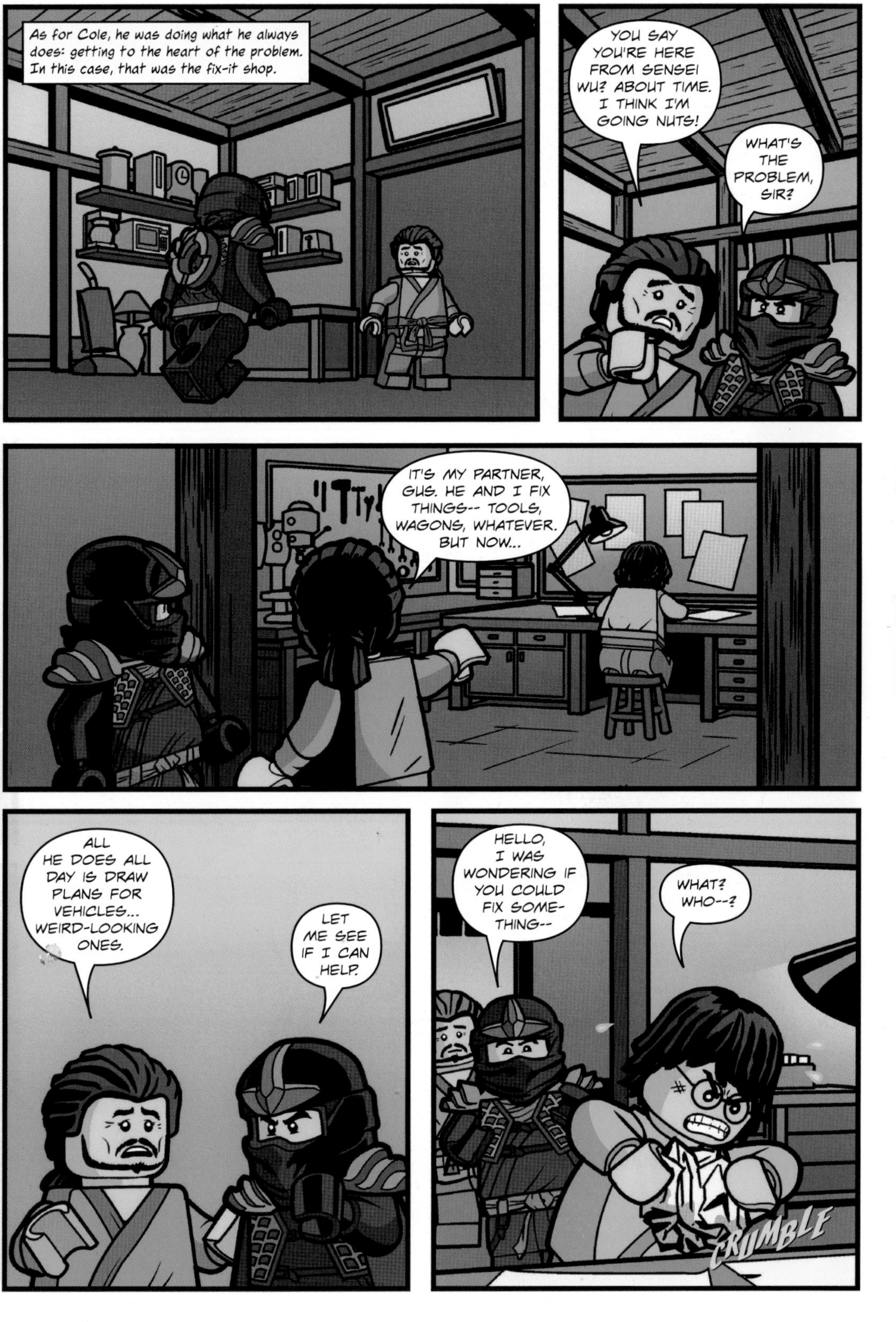
As for Cole, he was doing what he always does: getting to the heart of the problem. In this case, that was the fix-it shop.
YOU SAY YOU'RE HERE FROM SENSEI WU? ABOUT TIME. I THINK I'M GOING NUTS!
WHAT'S THE PROBLEM, SIR?
IT'S MY PARTNER, GUS. HE AND I FIX THINGS-- TOOLS, WAGONS, WHATEVER. BUT NOW...
ALL HE DOES ALL DAY IS DRAW PLANS FOR VEHICLES... WEIRD-LOOKING ONES.
LET ME SEE IF I CAN HELP.
HELLO, I WAS WONDERING IF YOU COULD FIX SOME-THING--
WHAT? WHO--?
CRUMBLE

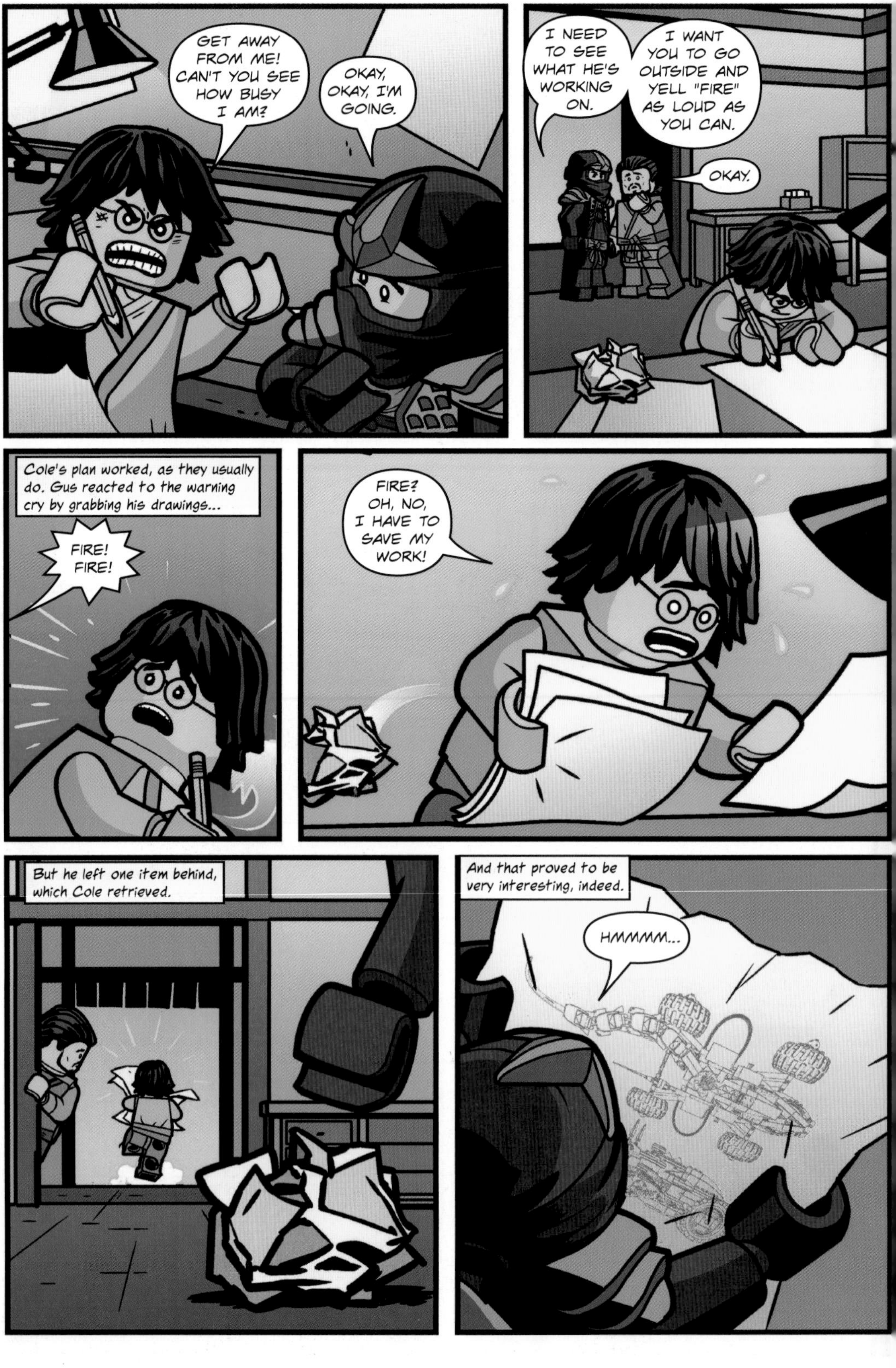
GET AWAY FROM ME! CAN'T YOU SEE HOW BUSY I AM?
OKAY, OKAY, I'M GOING.
I NEED TO SEE WHAT HE'S WORKING ON.
I WANT YOU TO GO OUTSIDE AND YELL "FIRE" AS LOUD AS YOU CAN.
OKAY.
Cole's plan worked, as they usually do. Gus reacted to the warning cry by grabbing his drawings...
FIRE! FIRE!
FIRE? OH, NO, I HAVE TO SAVE MY WORK!
But he left one item behind, which Cole retrieved.
And that proved to be very interesting, indeed.
HMMMM...

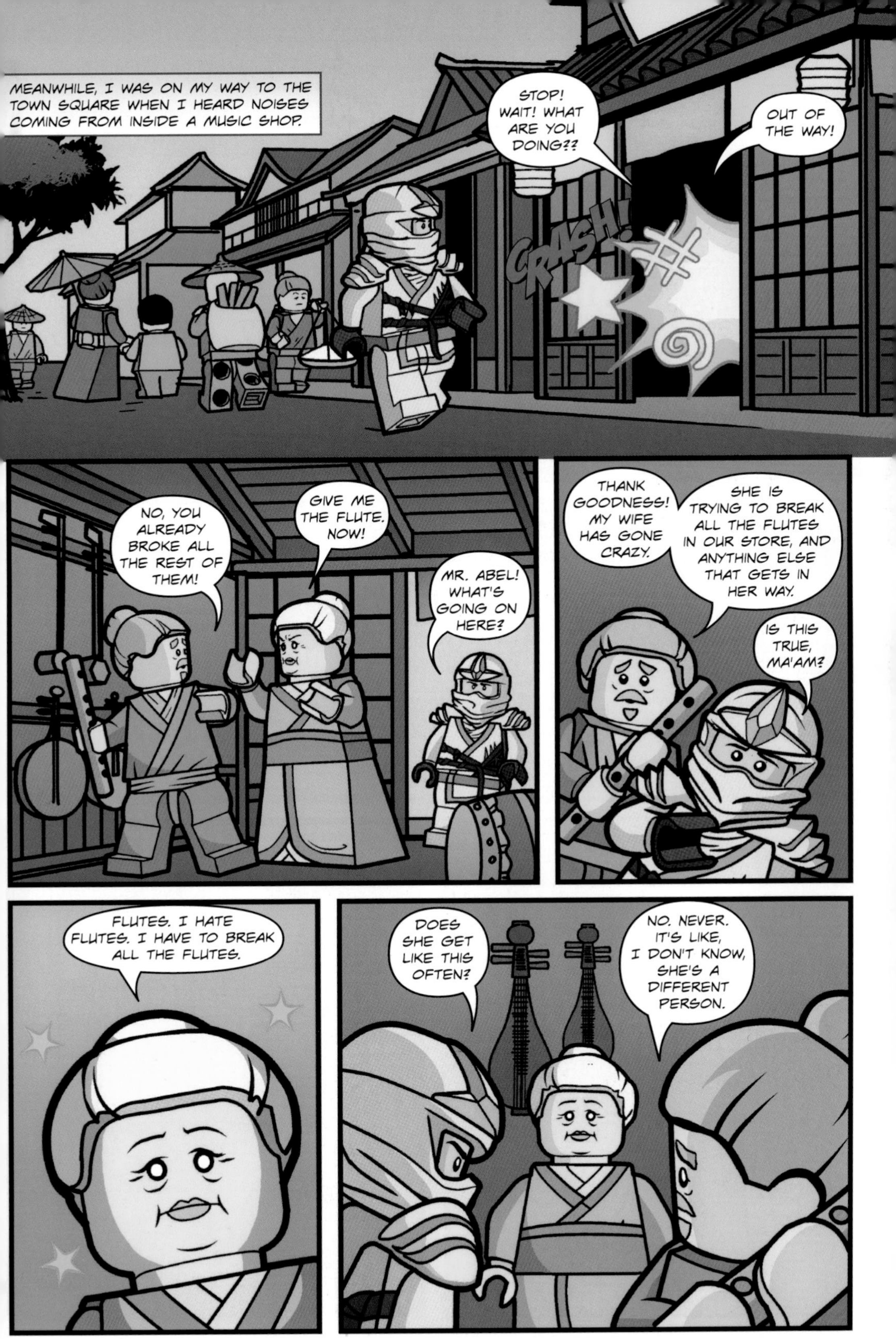
MEANWHILE, I WAS ON MY WAY TO THE TOWN SQUARE WHEN I HEARD NOISES COMING FROM INSIDE A MUSIC SHOP.
STOP! WAIT! WHAT ARE YOU DOING??
CRASH!
OUT OF THE WAY!
NO, YOU ALREADY BROKE ALL THE REST OF THEM!
GIVE ME THE FLUTE. NOW!
MR. ABEL! WHAT'S GOING ON HERE?
THANK GOODNESS! MY WIFE HAS GONE CRAZY.
SHE IS TRYING TO BREAK ALL THE FLUTES IN OUR STORE, AND ANYTHING ELSE THAT GETS IN HER WAY.
IS THIS TRUE, MA'AM?
FLUTES. I HATE FLUTES. I HAVE TO BREAK ALL THE FLUTES.
DOES SHE GET LIKE THIS OFTEN?
NO. NEVER. IT'S LIKE, I DON'T KNOW, SHE'S A DIFFERENT PERSON.

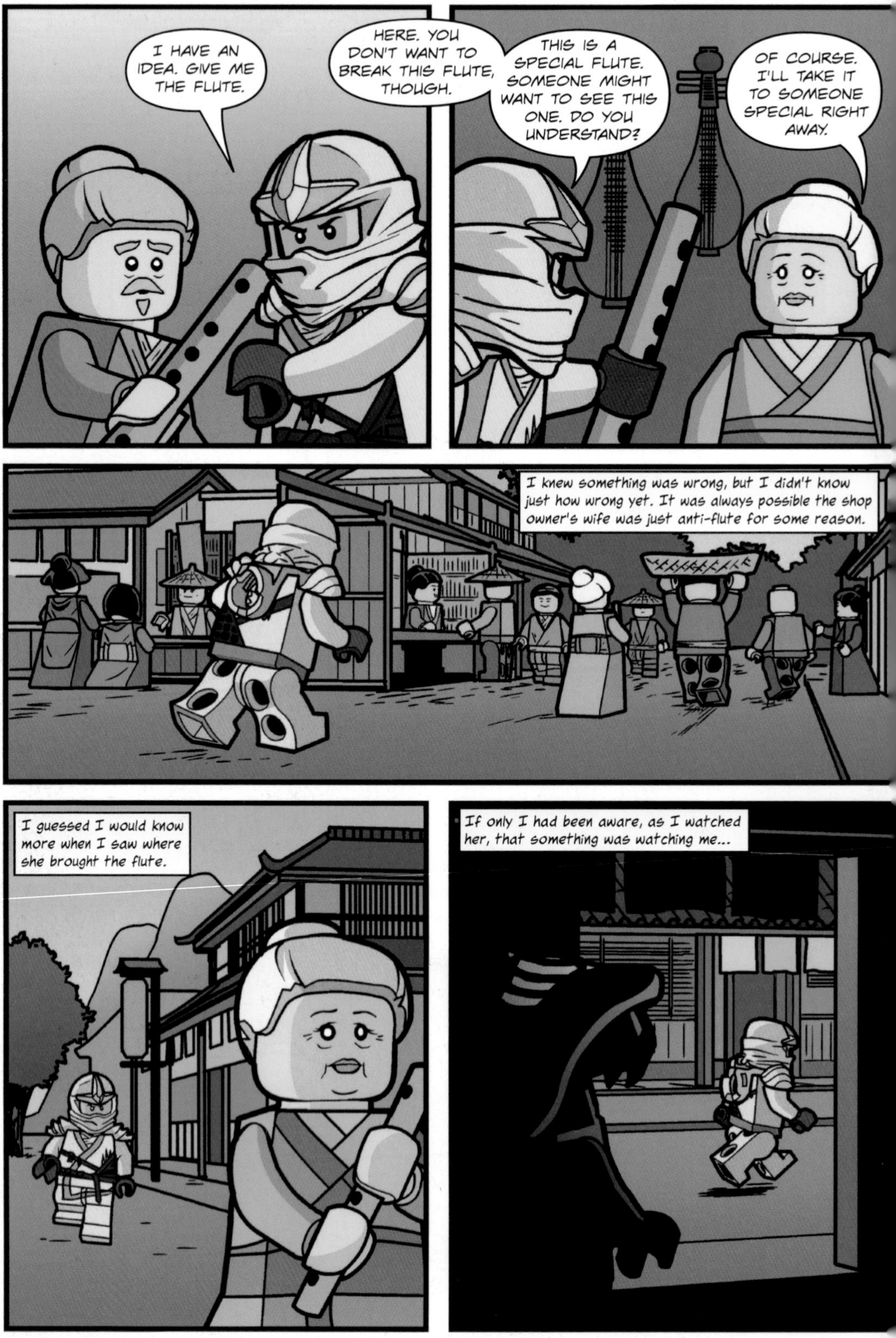
I HAVE AN IDEA. GIVE ME THE FLUTE.
HERE. YOU DON'T WANT TO BREAK THIS FLUTE, THOUGH.
THIS IS A SPECIAL FLUTE. SOMEONE MIGHT WANT TO SEE THIS ONE. DO YOU UNDERSTAND?
OF COURSE. I'LL TAKE IT TO SOMEONE SPECIAL RIGHT AWAY.
I knew something was wrong, but I didn't know just how wrong yet. It was always possible the shop owner's wife was just anti-flute for some reason.
I guessed I would know more when I saw where she brought the flute.
If only I had been aware, as I watched her, that something was watching me...

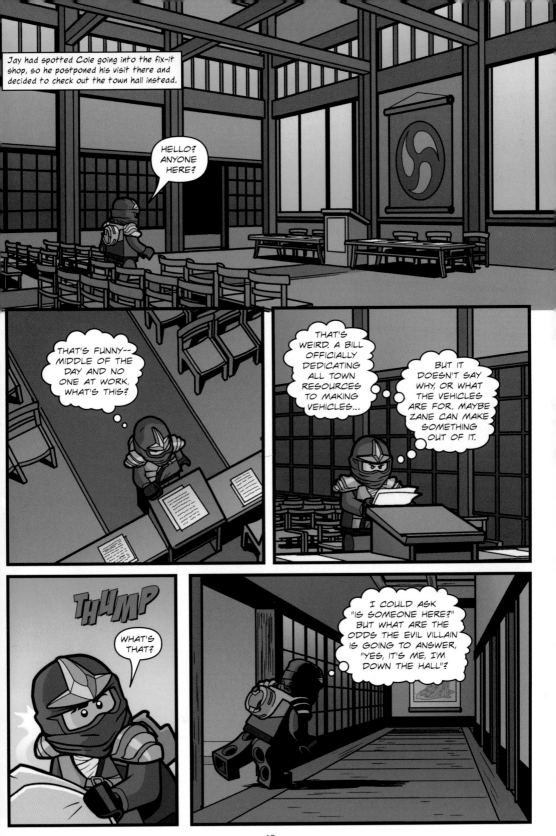

Jay had spotted Cole going into the fix-it shop, so he postponed his visit there and decided to check out the town hall instead.

HELLO? ANYONE HERE?

THAT'S FUNNY-- MIDDLE OF THE DAY AND NO ONE AT WORK. WHAT'S THIS?

THAT'S WEIRD. A BILL OFFICIALLY DEDICATING ALL TOWN RESOURCES TO MAKING VEHICLES...

BUT IT DOESN'T SAY WHY, OR WHAT THE VEHICLES ARE FOR. MAYBE ZANE CAN MAKE SOMETHING OUT OF IT.

THUMP

WHAT'S THAT?

I COULD ASK "IS SOMEONE HERE?" BUT WHAT ARE THE ODDS THE EVIL VILLAIN IS GOING TO ANSWER, "YES, IT'S ME, I'M DOWN THE HALL"?

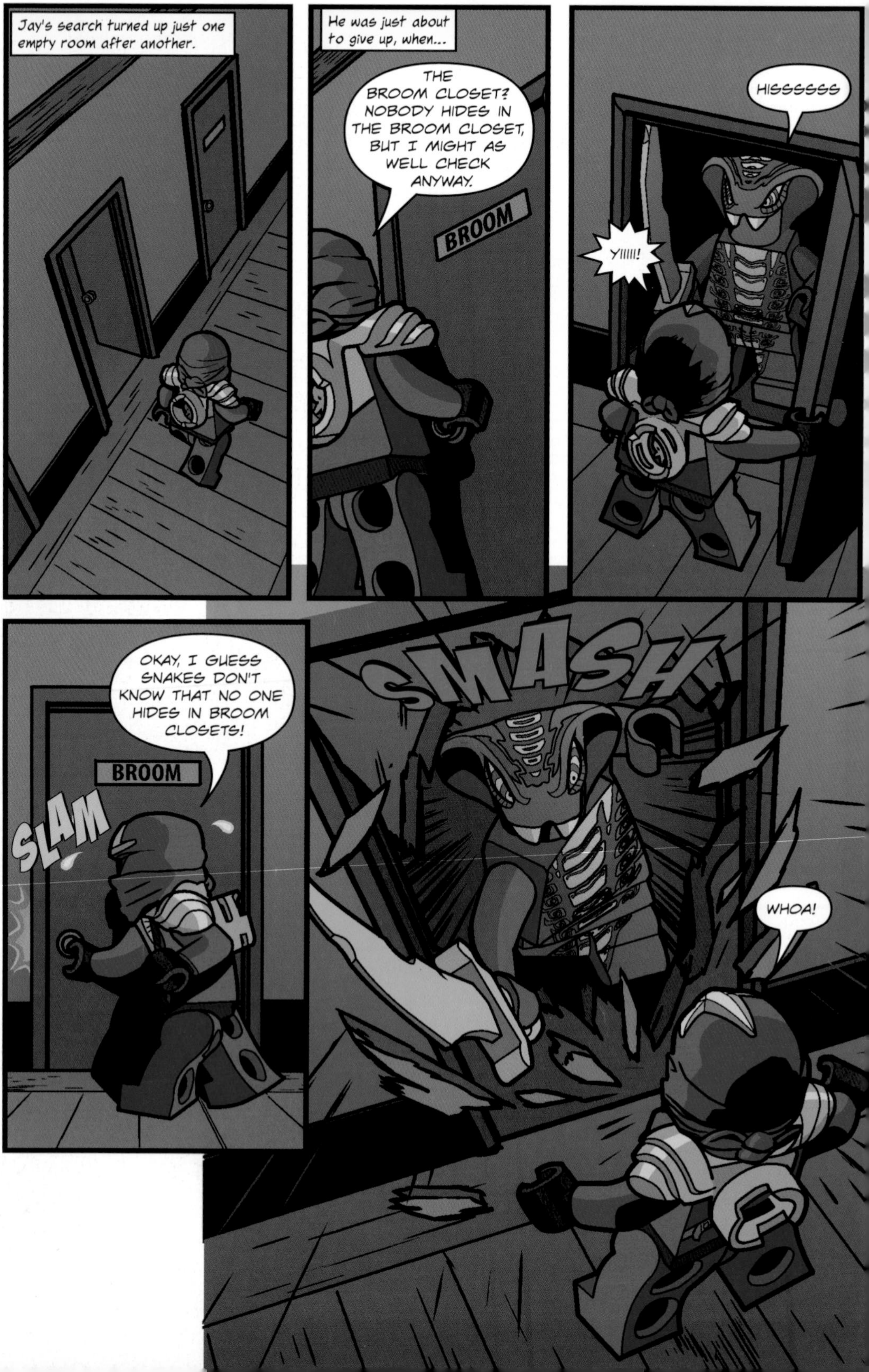
Jay's search turned up just one empty room after another.
He was just about to give up, when...
THE BROOM CLOSET? NOBODY HIDES IN THE BROOM CLOSET, BUT I MIGHT AS WELL CHECK ANYWAY.
BROOM
HISSSSSS
YIIIII!
OKAY, I GUESS SNAKES DON'T KNOW THAT NO ONE HIDES IN BROOM CLOSETS!
BROOM
SLAM
SMASH
WHOA!

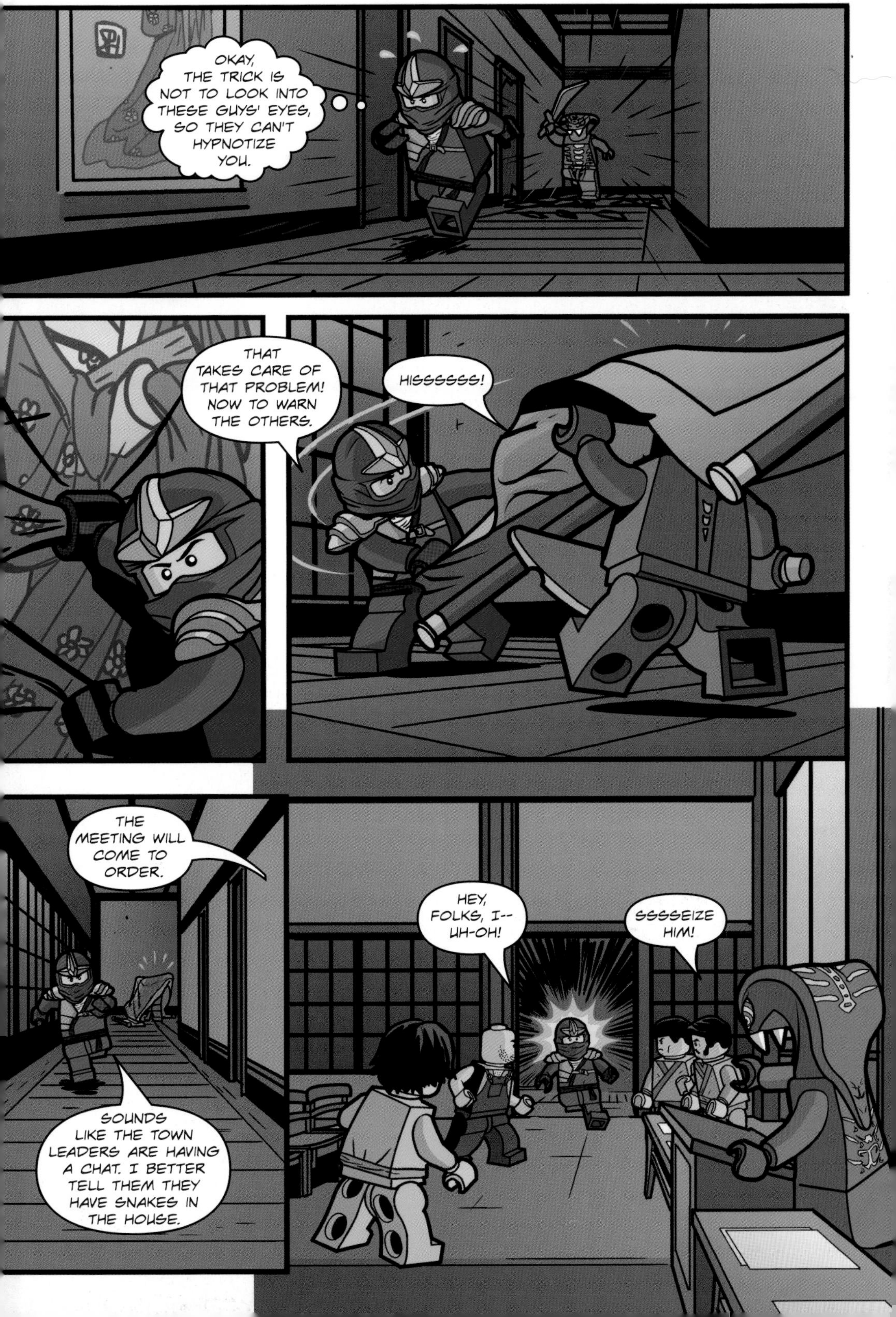
OKAY, THE TRICK IS NOT TO LOOK INTO THESE GUYS' EYES, SO THEY CAN'T HYPNOTIZE YOU.
THAT TAKES CARE OF THAT PROBLEM! NOW TO WARN THE OTHERS.
HISSSSSS!
THE MEETING WILL COME TO ORDER.
SOUNDS LIKE THE TOWN LEADERS ARE HAVING A CHAT. I BETTER TELL THEM THEY HAVE SNAKES IN THE HOUSE.
HEY, FOLKS, I-- UH-OH!
SSSSEIZE HIM!

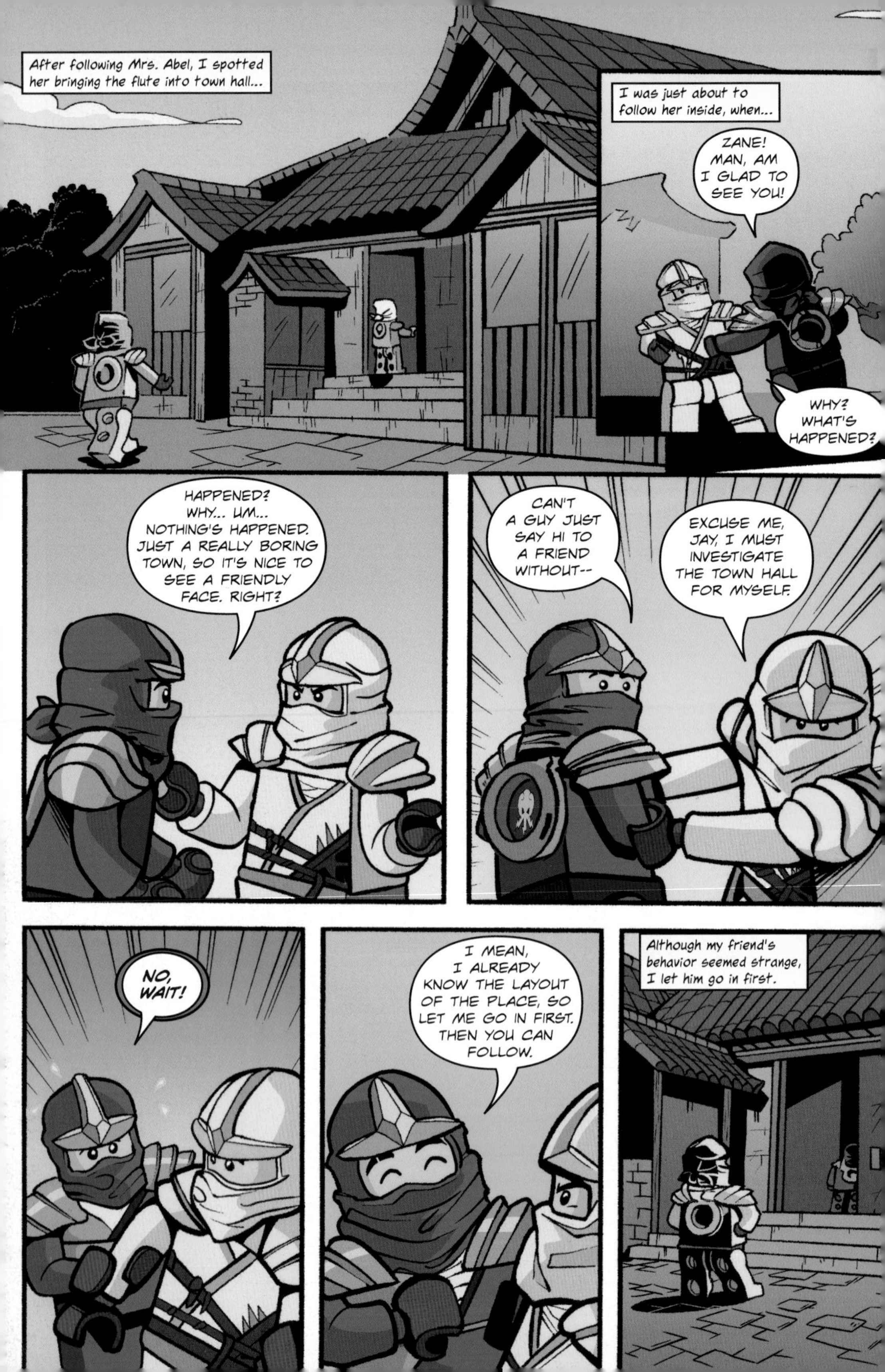
After following Mrs. Abel, I spotted her bringing the flute into town hall...
I was just about to follow her inside, when...
ZANE! MAN, AM I GLAD TO SEE YOU!
WHY? WHAT'S HAPPENED?
HAPPENED? WHY... UM... NOTHING'S HAPPENED. JUST A REALLY BORING TOWN, SO IT'S NICE TO SEE A FRIENDLY FACE. RIGHT?
CAN'T A GUY JUST SAY HI TO A FRIEND WITHOUT--
EXCUSE ME, JAY, I MUST INVESTIGATE THE TOWN HALL FOR MYSELF.
NO, WAIT!
I MEAN, I ALREADY KNOW THE LAYOUT OF THE PLACE, SO LET ME GO IN FIRST. THEN YOU CAN FOLLOW.
Although my friend's behavior seemed strange, I let him go in first.

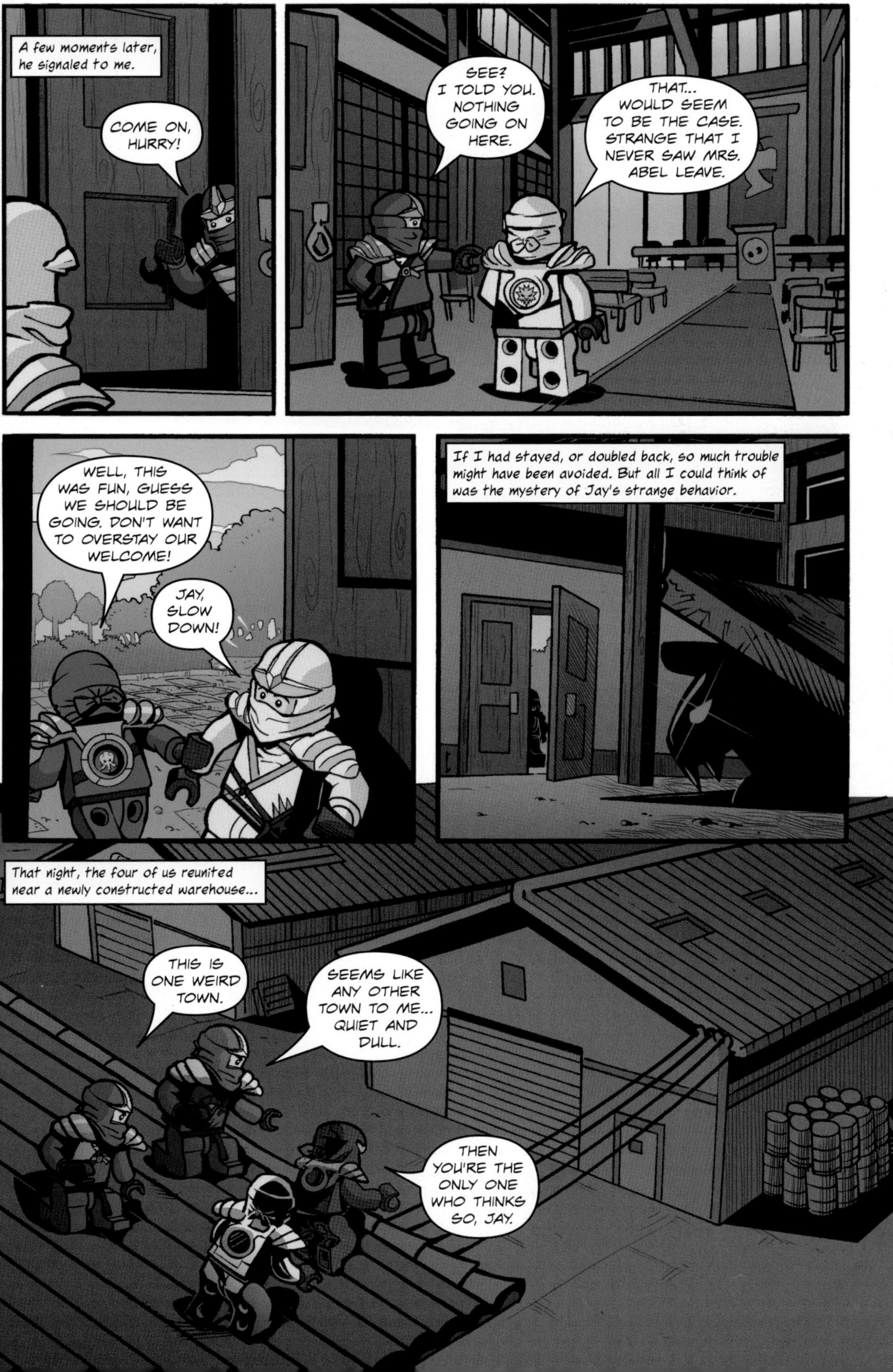
A few moments later, he signaled to me.
COME ON, HURRY!
SEE? I TOLD YOU. NOTHING GOING ON HERE.
THAT... WOULD SEEM TO BE THE CASE. STRANGE THAT I NEVER SAW MRS. ABEL LEAVE.
WELL, THIS WAS FUN, GUESS WE SHOULD BE GOING. DON'T WANT TO OVERSTAY OUR WELCOME!
JAY, SLOW DOWN!
If I had stayed, or doubled back, so much trouble might have been avoided. But all I could think of was the mystery of Jay's strange behavior.
That night, the four of us reunited near a newly constructed warehouse...
THIS IS ONE WEIRD TOWN.
SEEMS LIKE ANY OTHER TOWN TO ME... QUIET AND DULL.
THEN YOU'RE THE ONLY ONE WHO THINKS SO, JAY.

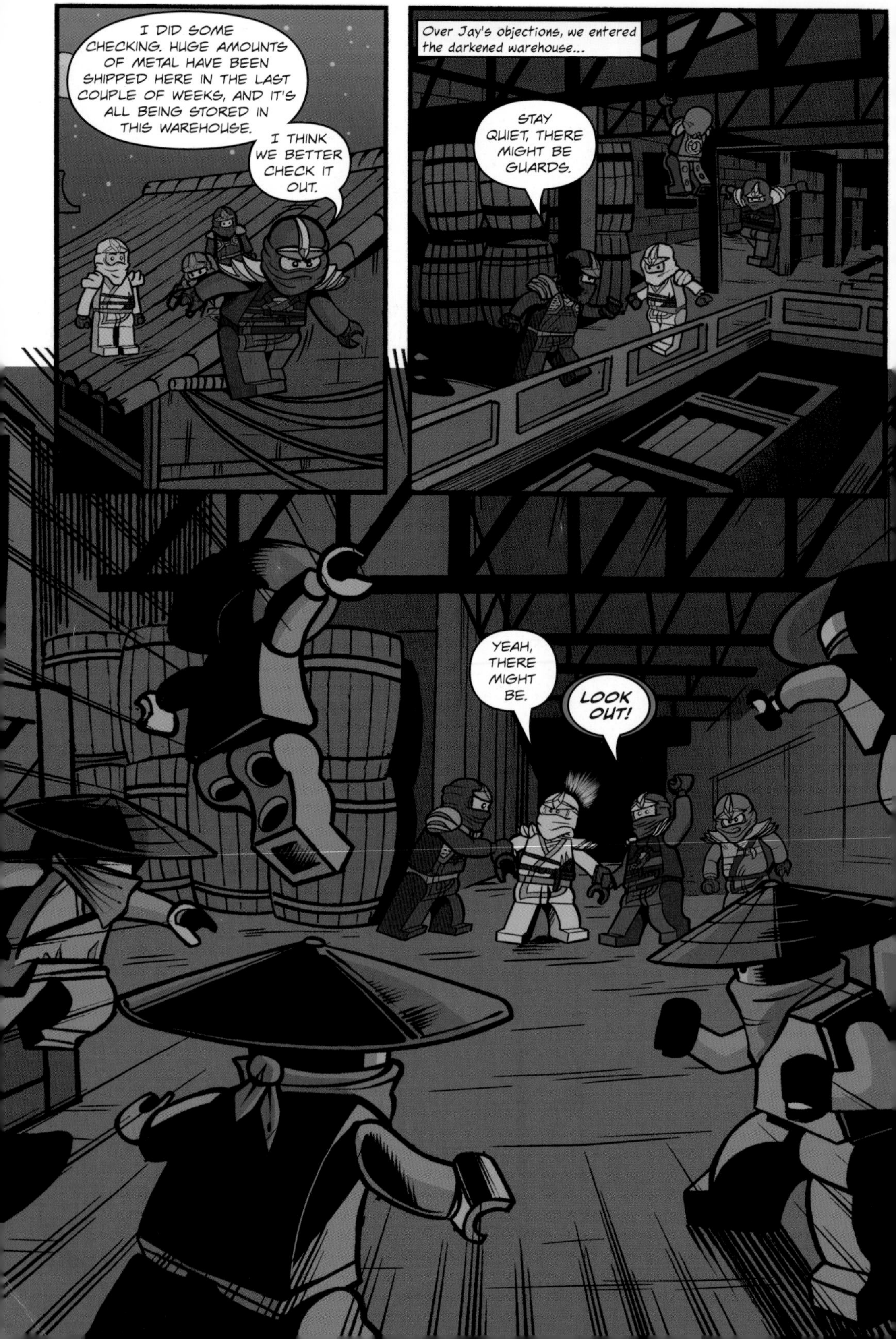
I DID SOME CHECKING. HUGE AMOUNTS OF METAL HAVE BEEN SHIPPED HERE IN THE LAST COUPLE OF WEEKS, AND IT'S ALL BEING STORED IN THIS WAREHOUSE.
I THINK WE BETTER CHECK IT OUT.
Over Jay's objections, we entered the darkened warehouse...
STAY QUIET, THERE MIGHT BE GUARDS.
YEAH, THERE MIGHT BE.
LOOK OUT!

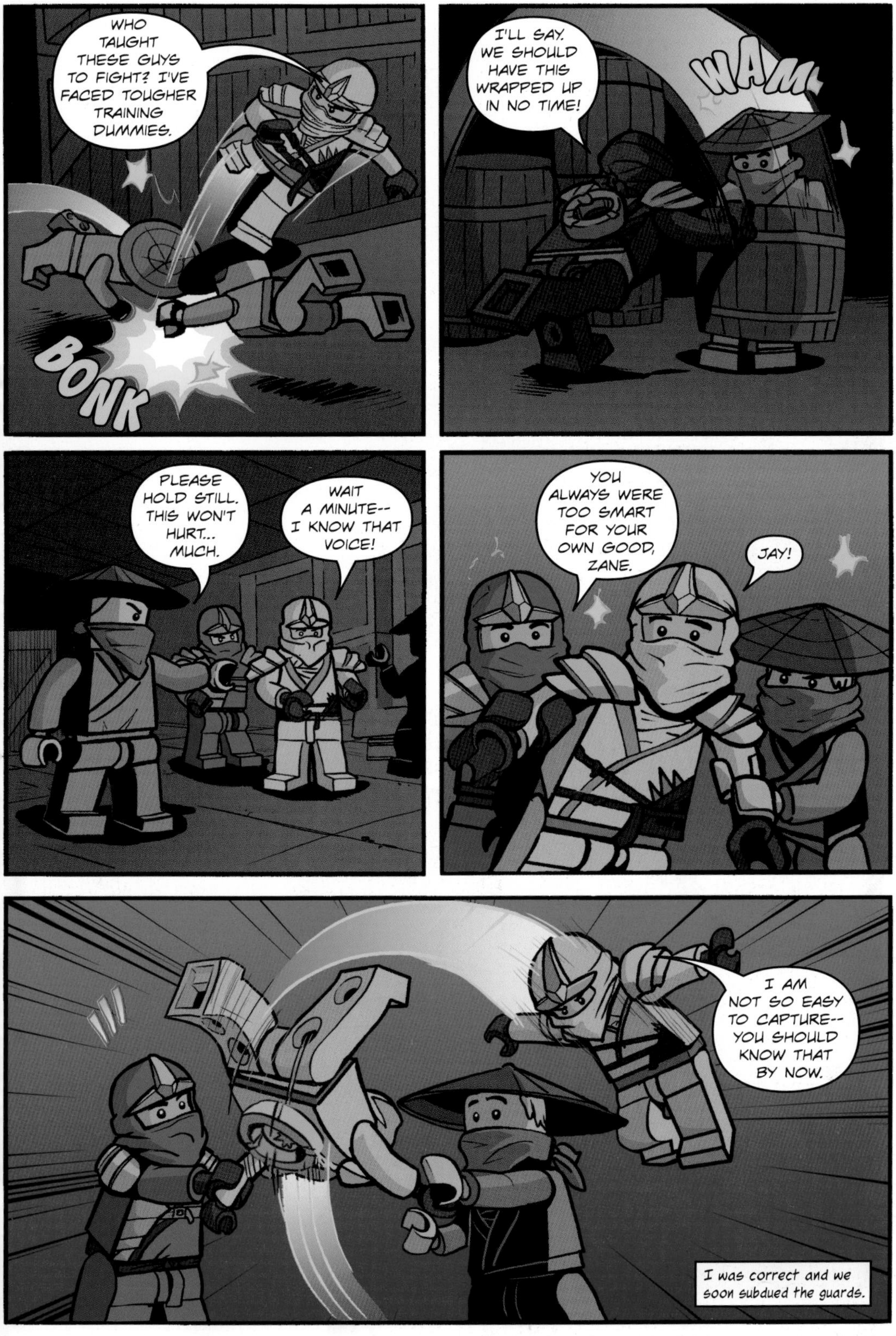
WHO TAUGHT THESE GUYS TO FIGHT? I'VE FACED TOUGHER TRAINING DUMMIES.
BONK
I'LL SAY. WE SHOULD HAVE THIS WRAPPED UP IN NO TIME!
WAM
PLEASE HOLD STILL. THIS WON'T HURT... MUCH.
WAIT A MINUTE-- I KNOW THAT VOICE!
YOU ALWAYS WERE TOO SMART FOR YOUR OWN GOOD, ZANE.
JAY!
I AM NOT SO EASY TO CAPTURE-- YOU SHOULD KNOW THAT BY NOW.
I was correct and we soon subdued the guards.

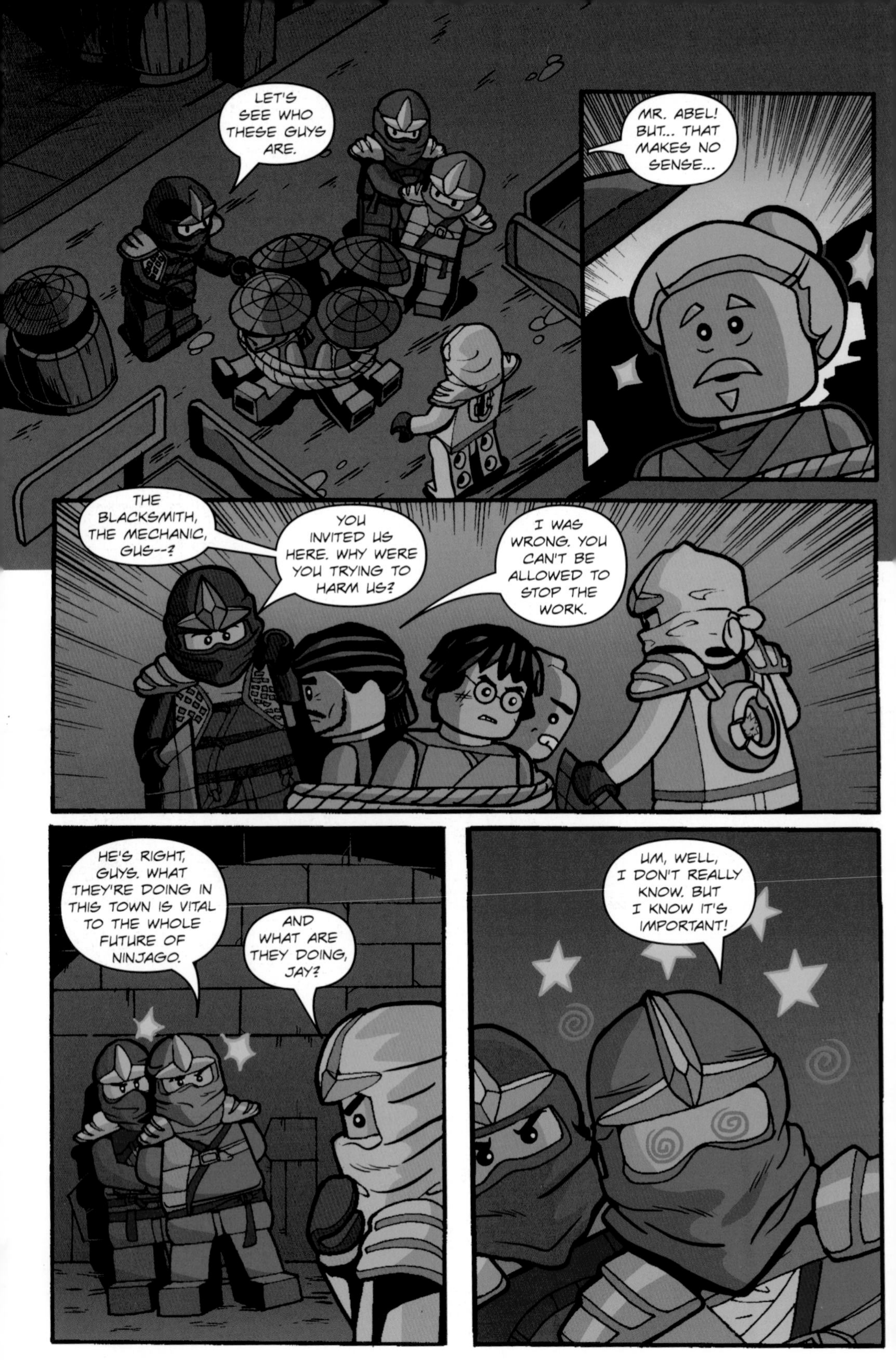
LET'S SEE WHO THESE GUYS ARE.
MR. ABEL! BUT... THAT MAKES NO SENSE...
THE BLACKSMITH, THE MECHANIC, GUS--?
YOU INVITED US HERE. WHY WERE YOU TRYING TO HARM US?
I WAS WRONG. YOU CAN'T BE ALLOWED TO STOP THE WORK.
HE'S RIGHT, GUYS. WHAT THEY'RE DOING IN THIS TOWN IS VITAL TO THE WHOLE FUTURE OF NINJAGO.
AND WHAT ARE THEY DOING, JAY?
UM, WELL, I DON'T REALLY KNOW. BUT I KNOW IT'S IMPORTANT!

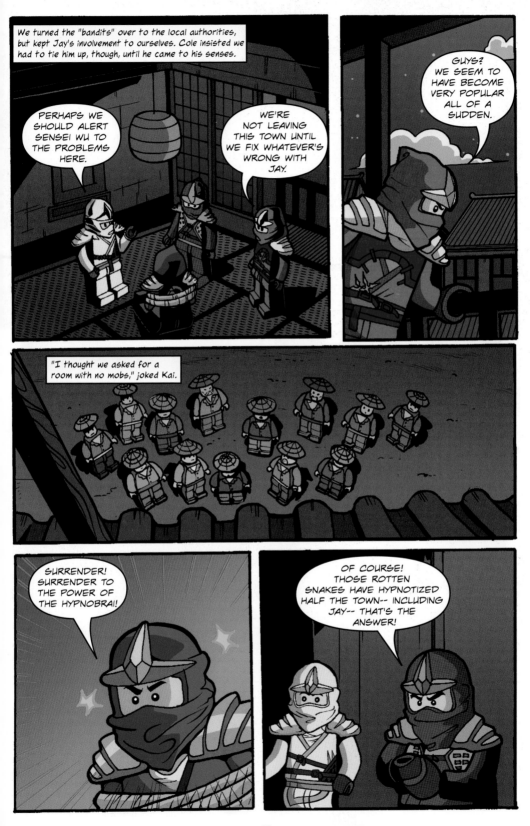

We turned the "bandits" over to the local authorities, but kept Jay's involvement to ourselves. Cole insisted we had to tie him up, though, until he came to his senses.

PERHAPS WE SHOULD ALERT SENSEI WU TO THE PROBLEMS HERE.

WE'RE NOT LEAVING THIS TOWN UNTIL WE FIX WHATEVER'S WRONG WITH JAY.

GUYS? WE SEEM TO HAVE BECOME VERY POPULAR ALL OF A SUDDEN.

"I thought we asked for a room with no mobs," joked Kai.

SURRENDER! SURRENDER TO THE POWER OF THE HYPNOBRAI!

OF COURSE! THOSE ROTTEN SNAKES HAVE HYPNOTIZED HALF THE TOWN-- INCLUDING JAY-- THAT'S THE ANSWER!

27

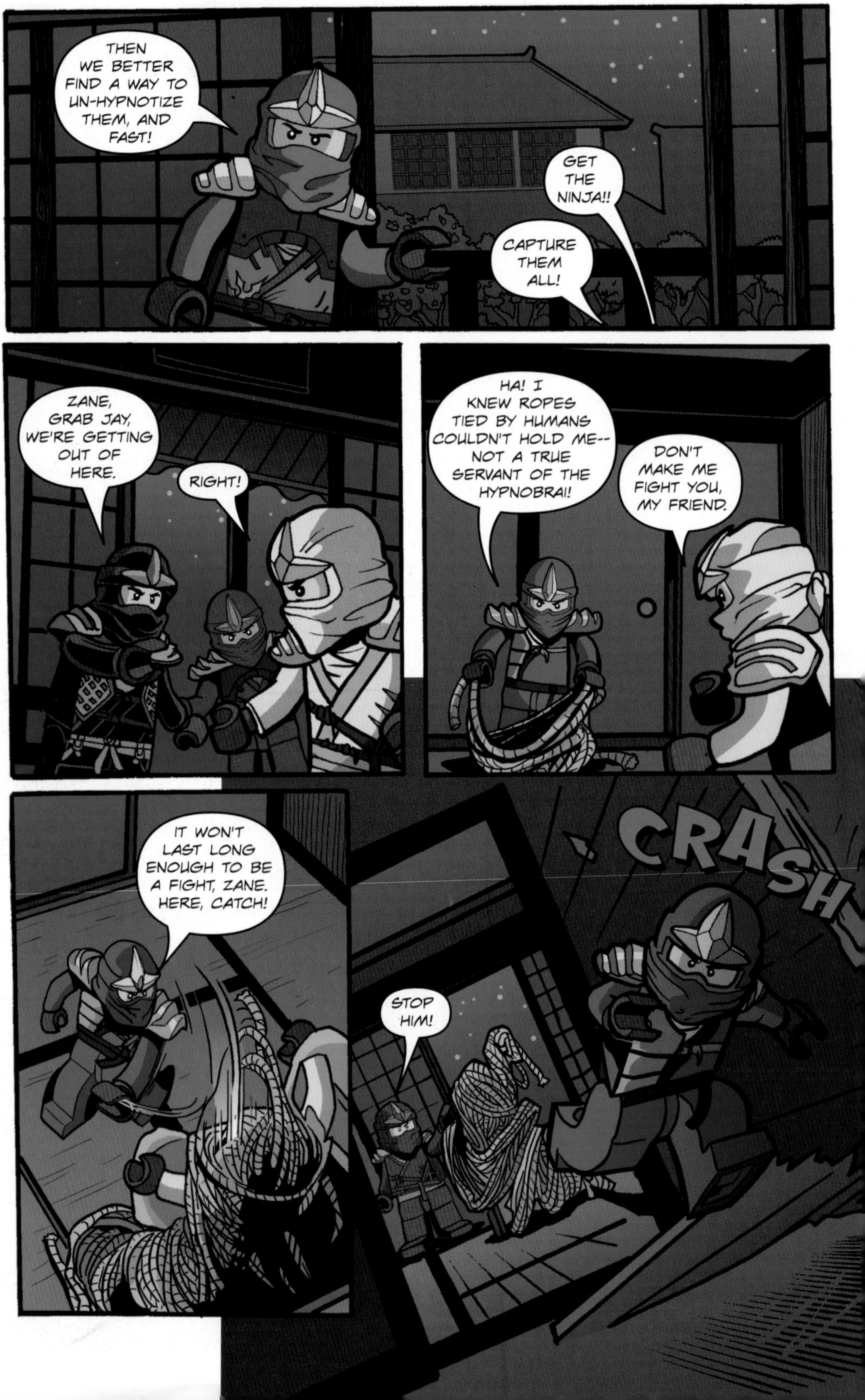

THEN WE BETTER FIND A WAY TO UN-HYPNOTIZE THEM, AND FAST!
GET THE NINJA!!
CAPTURE THEM ALL!
ZANE, GRAB JAY, WE'RE GETTING OUT OF HERE.
RIGHT!
HA! I KNEW ROPES TIED BY HUMANS COULDN'T HOLD ME-- NOT A TRUE SERVANT OF THE HYPNOBRAI!
DON'T MAKE ME FIGHT YOU, MY FRIEND.
IT WON'T LAST LONG ENOUGH TO BE A FIGHT, ZANE. HERE, CATCH!
CRASH
STOP HIM!

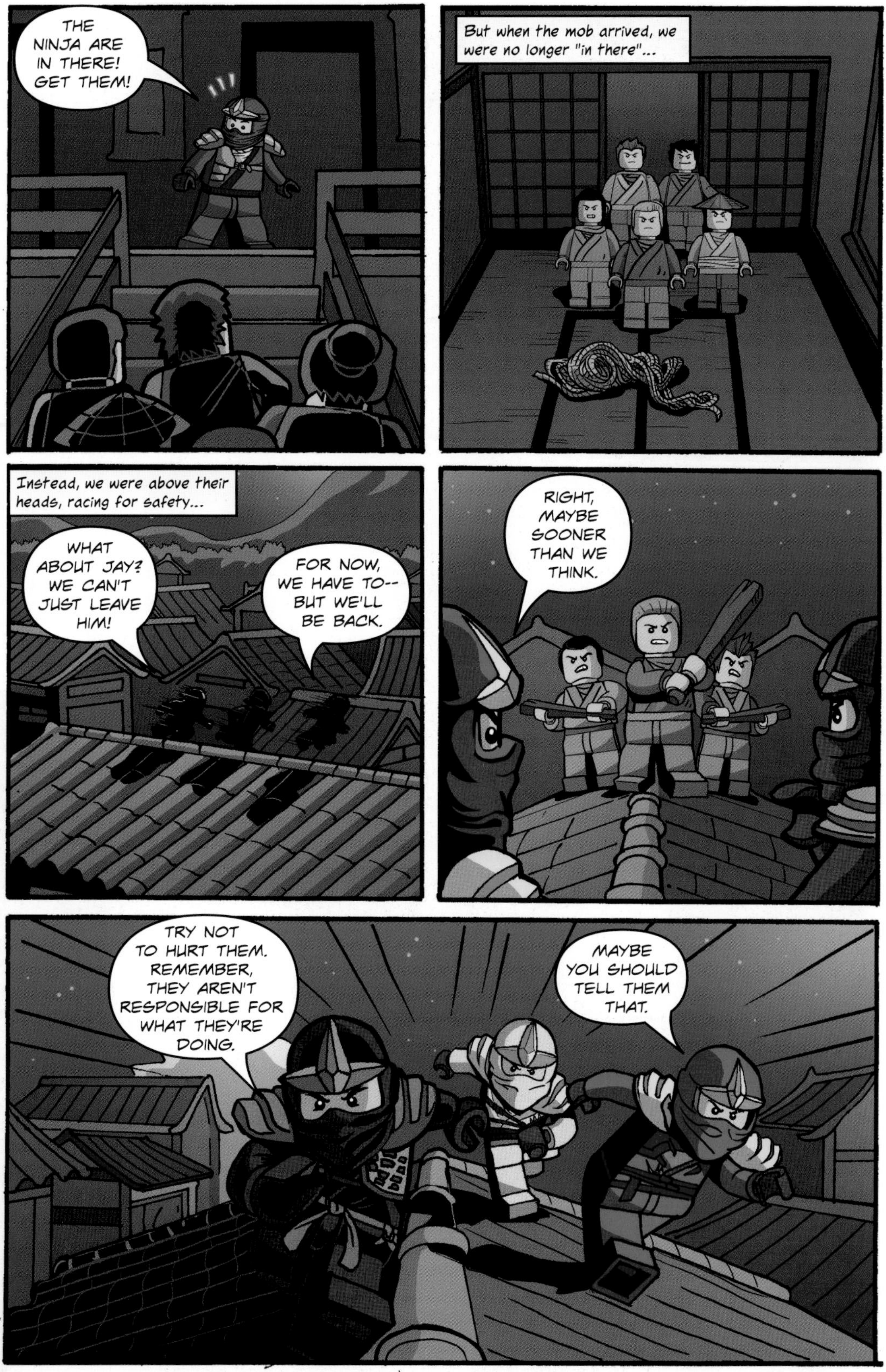
THE NINJA ARE IN THERE! GET THEM!
But when the mob arrived, we were no longer "in there"...
Instead, we were above their heads, racing for safety...
WHAT ABOUT JAY? WE CAN'T JUST LEAVE HIM!
FOR NOW, WE HAVE TO-- BUT WE'LL BE BACK.
RIGHT, MAYBE SOONER THAN WE THINK.
TRY NOT TO HURT THEM. REMEMBER, THEY AREN'T RESPONSIBLE FOR WHAT THEY'RE DOING.
MAYBE YOU SHOULD TELL THEM THAT.

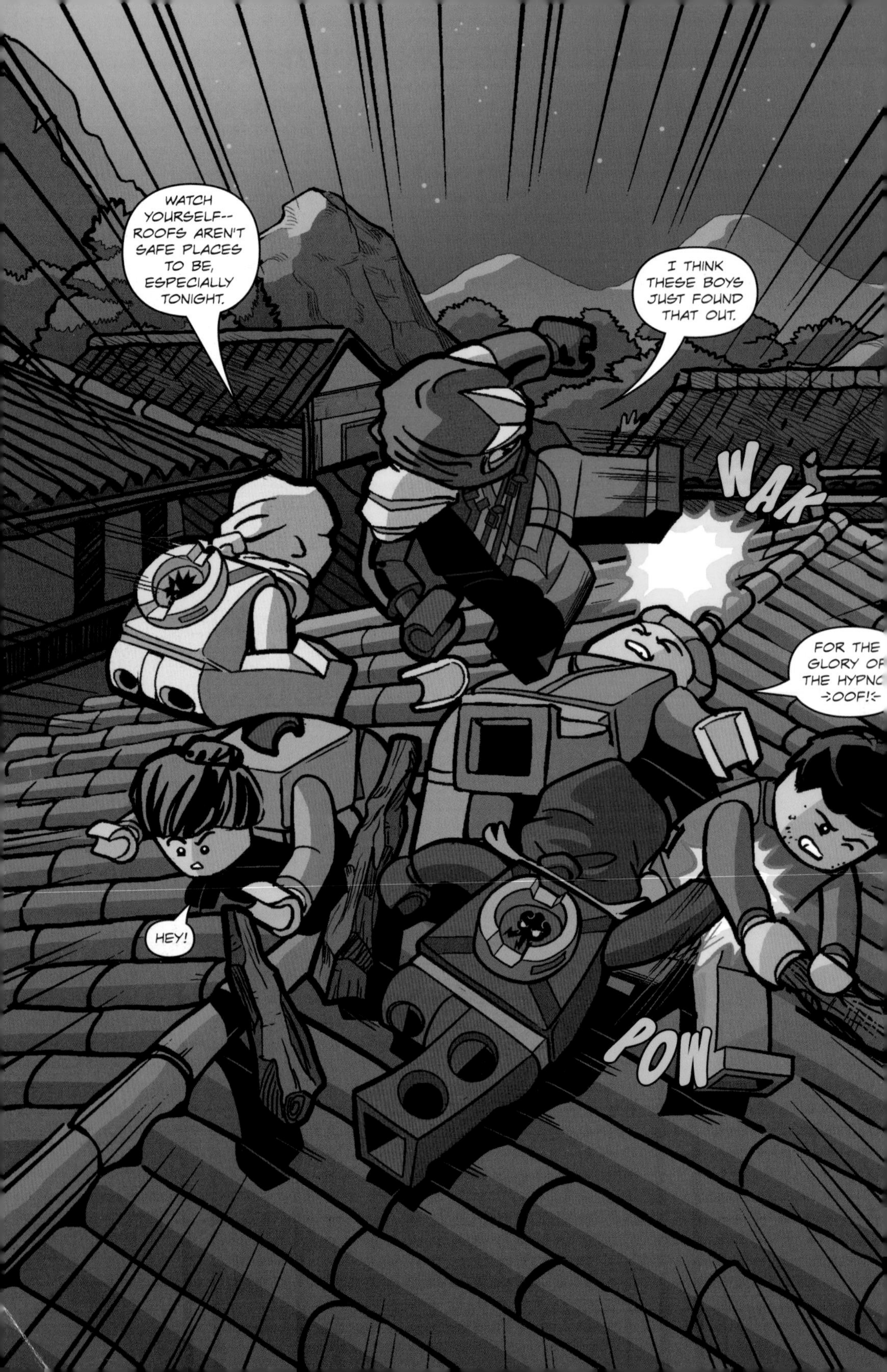
WATCH YOURSELF-- ROOFS AREN'T SAFE PLACES TO BE, ESPECIALLY TONIGHT.
I THINK THESE BOYS JUST FOUND THAT OUT.
WAK
FOR THE GLORY OF THE HYPNO -OOF!-
HEY!
POW

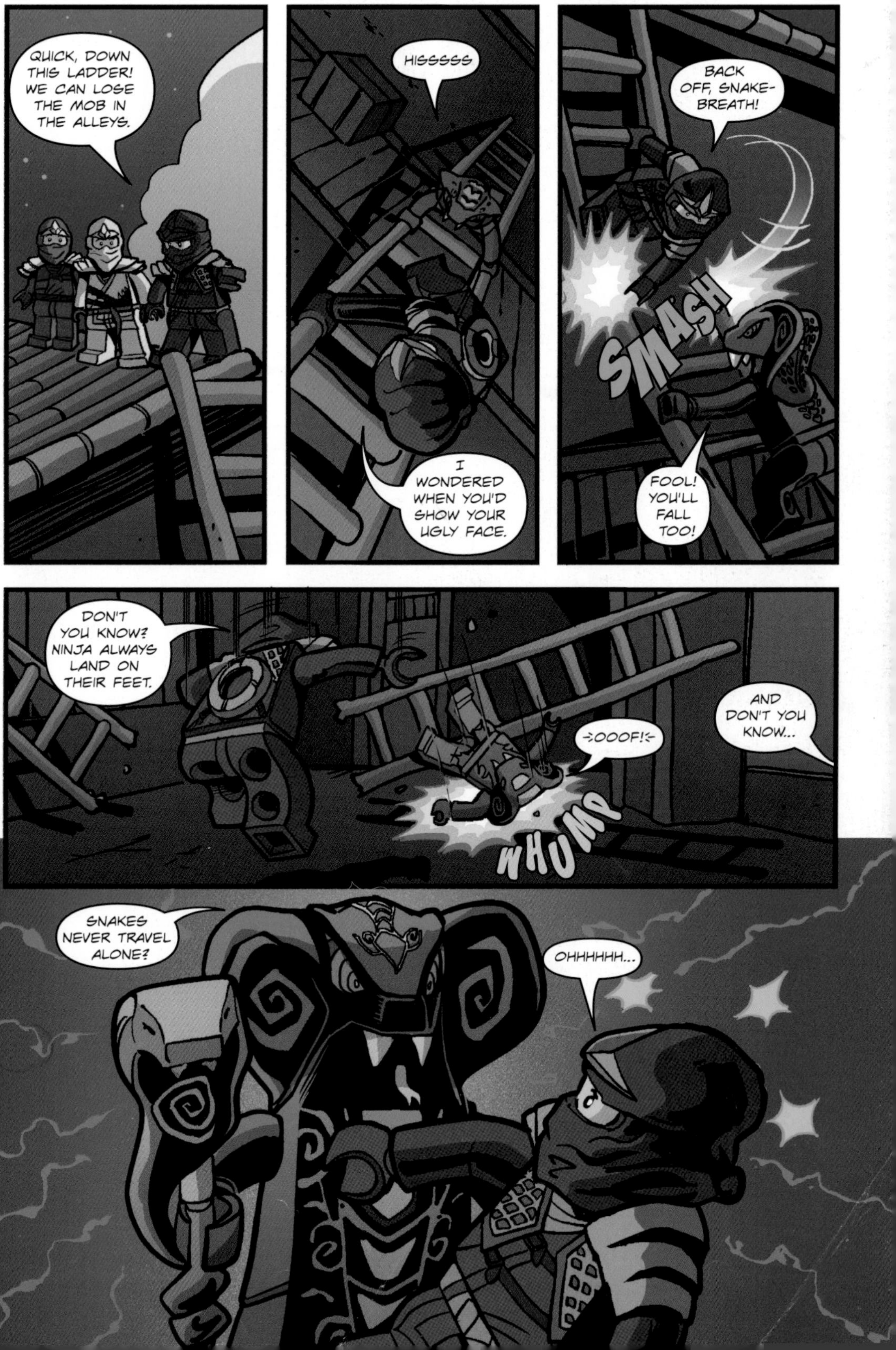
QUICK, DOWN THIS LADDER! WE CAN LOSE THE MOB IN THE ALLEYS.
HISSSSS
I WONDERED WHEN YOU'D SHOW YOUR UGLY FACE.
BACK OFF, SNAKE-BREATH!
SMASH
FOOL! YOU'LL FALL TOO!
DON'T YOU KNOW? NINJA ALWAYS LAND ON THEIR FEET.
OOOF!
WHUMP
AND DON'T YOU KNOW...
SNAKES NEVER TRAVEL ALONE?
OHHHHHH...

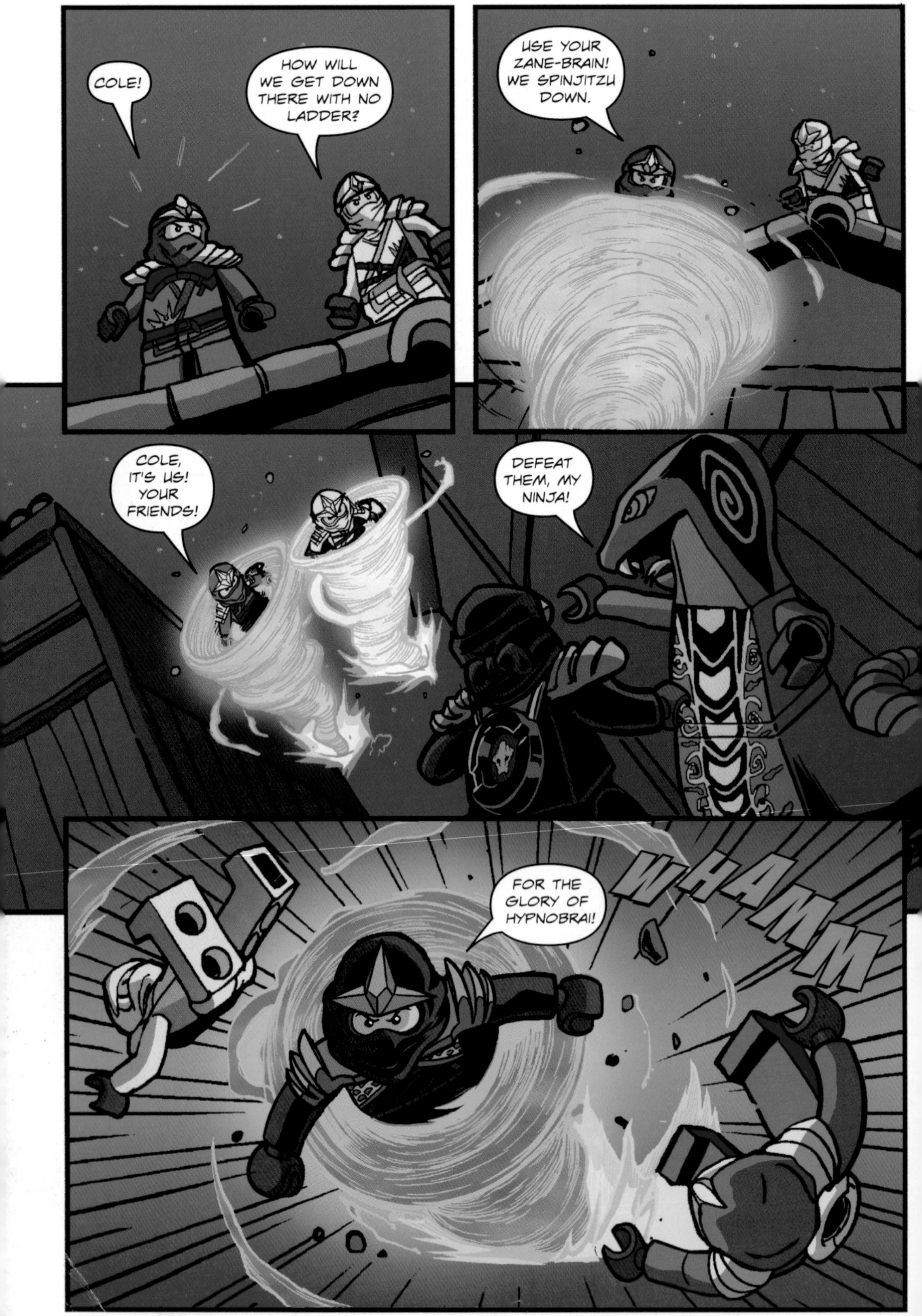
COLE!
HOW WILL WE GET DOWN THERE WITH NO LADDER?
USE YOUR ZANE-BRAIN! WE SPINJITZU DOWN.
COLE, IT'S US! YOUR FRIENDS!
DEFEAT THEM, MY NINJA!
WHAMM
FOR THE GLORY OF HYPNOBRAI!

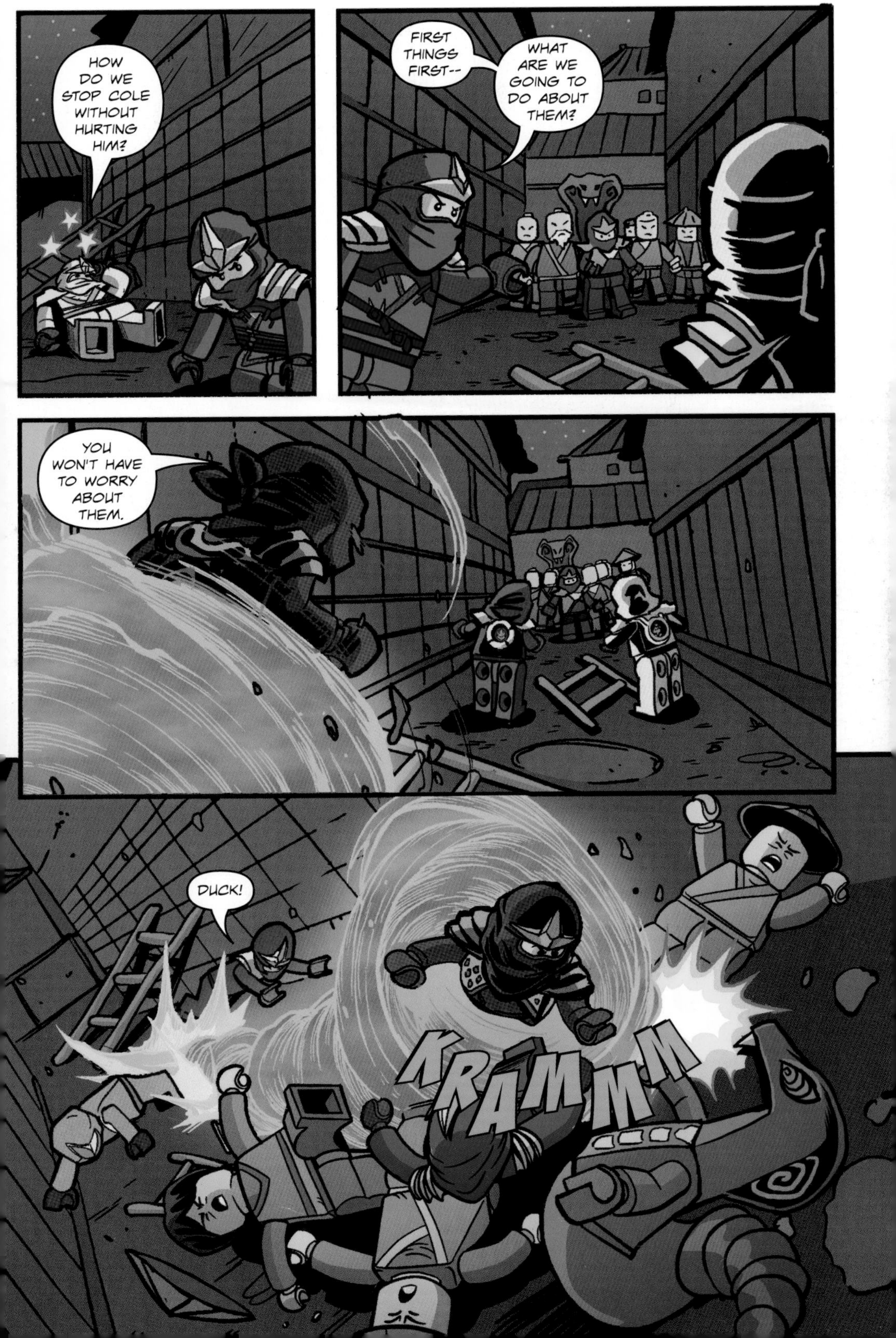
HOW DO WE STOP COLE WITHOUT HURTING HIM?
FIRST THINGS FIRST--
WHAT ARE WE GOING TO DO ABOUT THEM?
YOU WON'T HAVE TO WORRY ABOUT THEM.
DUCK!
KRAMMM

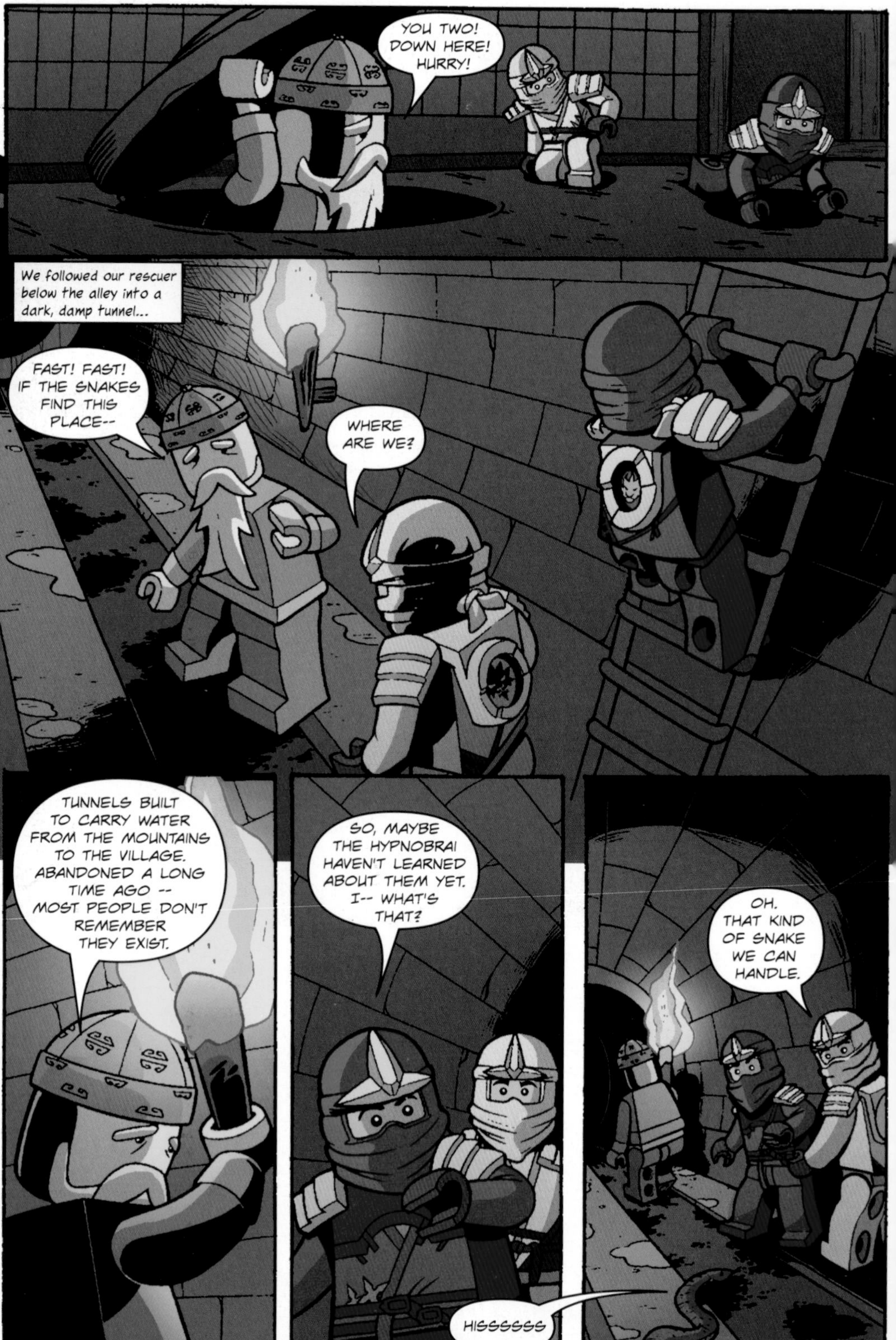
YOU TWO! DOWN HERE! HURRY!
We followed our rescuer below the alley into a dark, damp tunnel...
FAST! FAST! IF THE SNAKES FIND THIS PLACE--
WHERE ARE WE?
TUNNELS BUILT TO CARRY WATER FROM THE MOUNTAINS TO THE VILLAGE. ABANDONED A LONG TIME AGO -- MOST PEOPLE DON'T REMEMBER THEY EXIST.
SO, MAYBE THE HYPNOBRAI HAVEN'T LEARNED ABOUT THEM YET. I-- WHAT'S THAT?
HISSSSSS
OH. THAT KIND OF SNAKE WE CAN HANDLE.

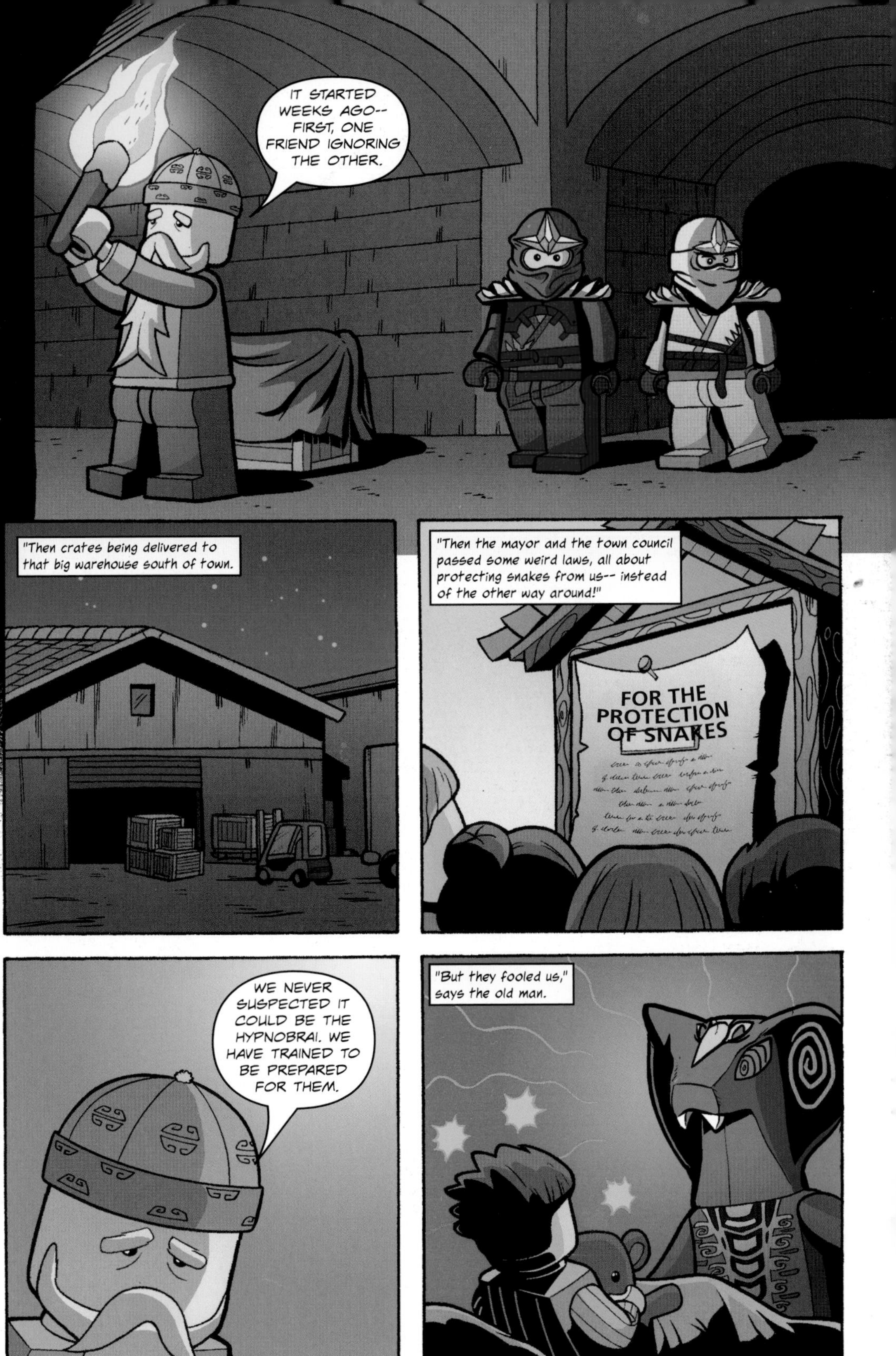
IT STARTED WEEKS AGO-- FIRST, ONE FRIEND IGNORING THE OTHER.
"Then crates being delivered to that big warehouse south of town.
"Then the mayor and the town council passed some weird laws, all about protecting snakes from us-- instead of the other way around!"
FOR THE PROTECTION OF SNAKES
WE NEVER SUSPECTED IT COULD BE THE HYPNOBRAI. WE HAVE TRAINED TO BE PREPARED FOR THEM.
"But they fooled us," says the old man.

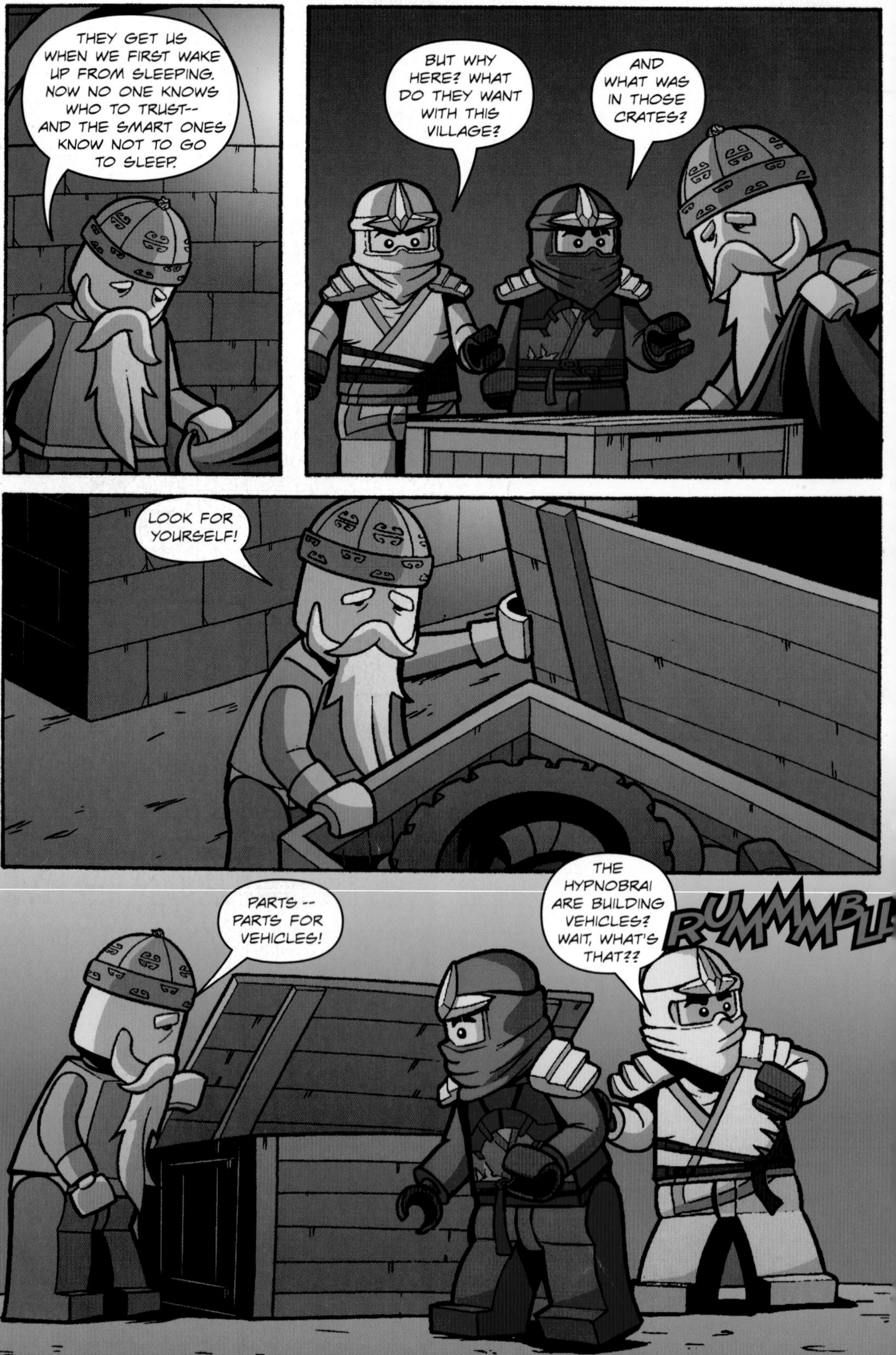
THEY GET US WHEN WE FIRST WAKE UP FROM SLEEPING. NOW NO ONE KNOWS WHO TO TRUST-- AND THE SMART ONES KNOW NOT TO GO TO SLEEP.
BUT WHY HERE? WHAT DO THEY WANT WITH THIS VILLAGE?
AND WHAT WAS IN THOSE CRATES?
LOOK FOR YOURSELF!
PARTS -- PARTS FOR VEHICLES!
THE HYPNOBRAI ARE BUILDING VEHICLES? WAIT, WHAT'S THAT??
RUMMMBL

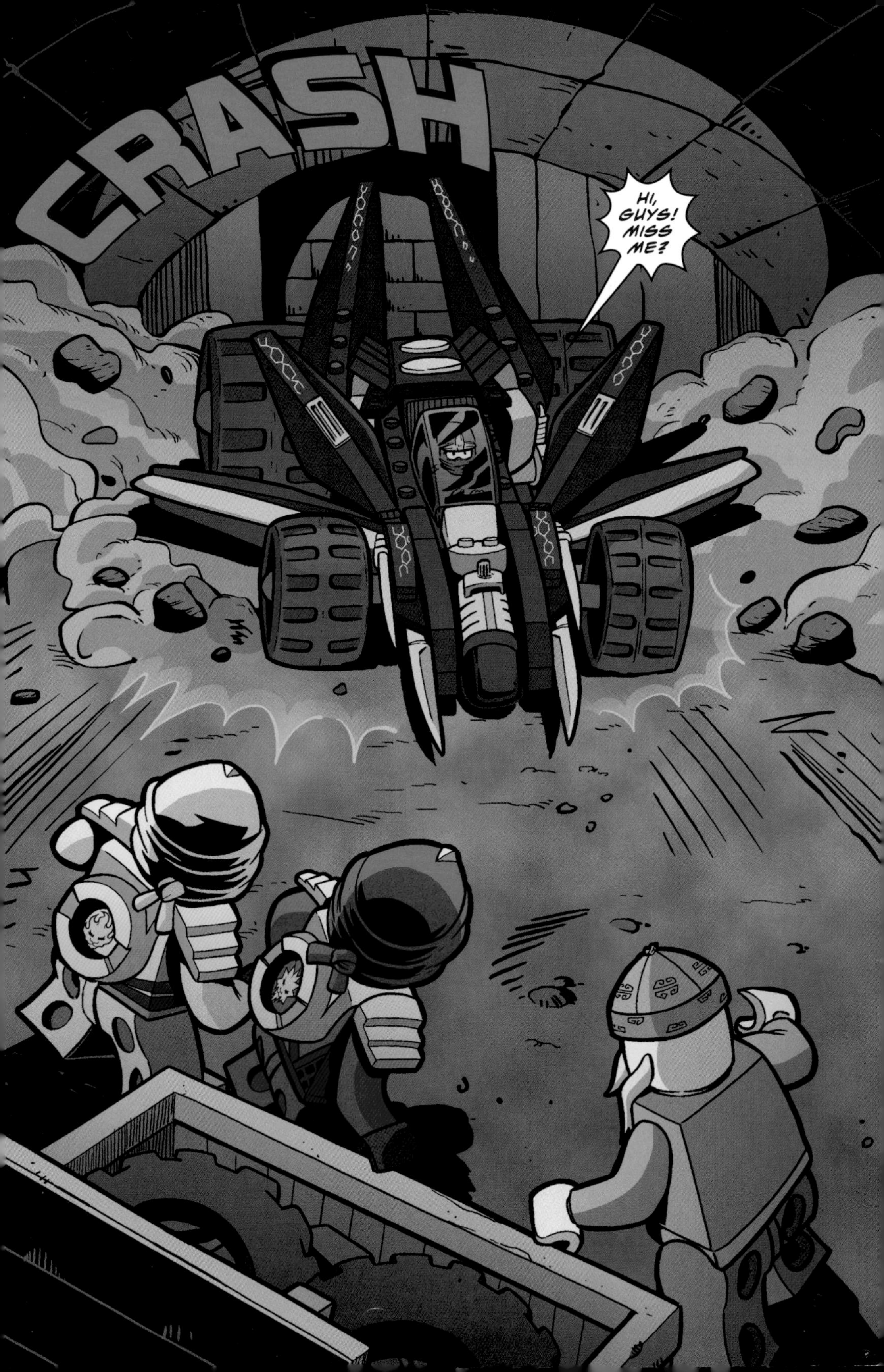
CRASH
HI, GUYS! MISS ME?

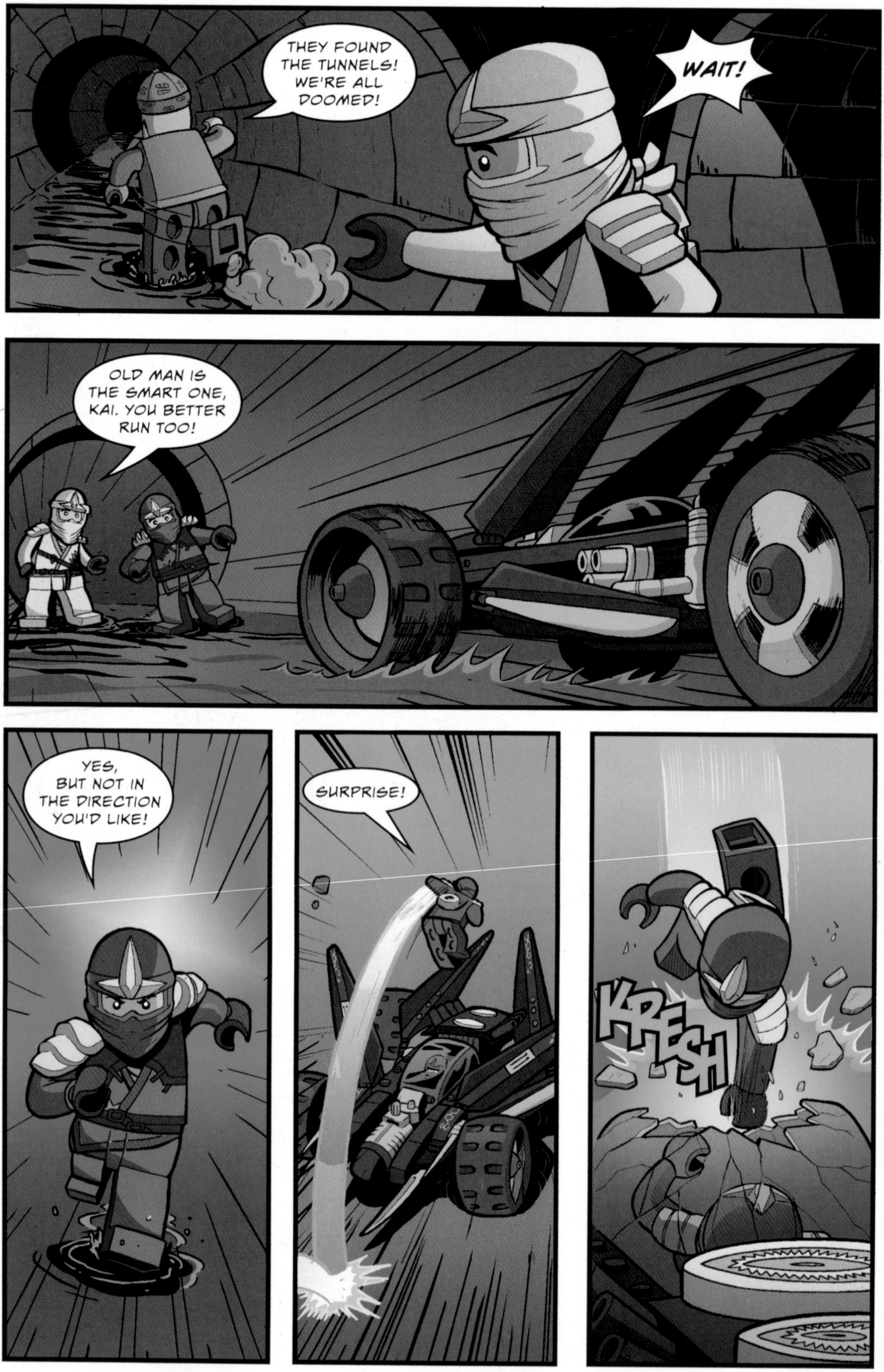
THEY FOUND THE TUNNELS! WE'RE ALL DOOMED!
WAIT!
OLD MAN IS THE SMART ONE, KAI. YOU BETTER RUN TOO!
YES, BUT NOT IN THE DIRECTION YOU'D LIKE!
SURPRISE!
KRESH

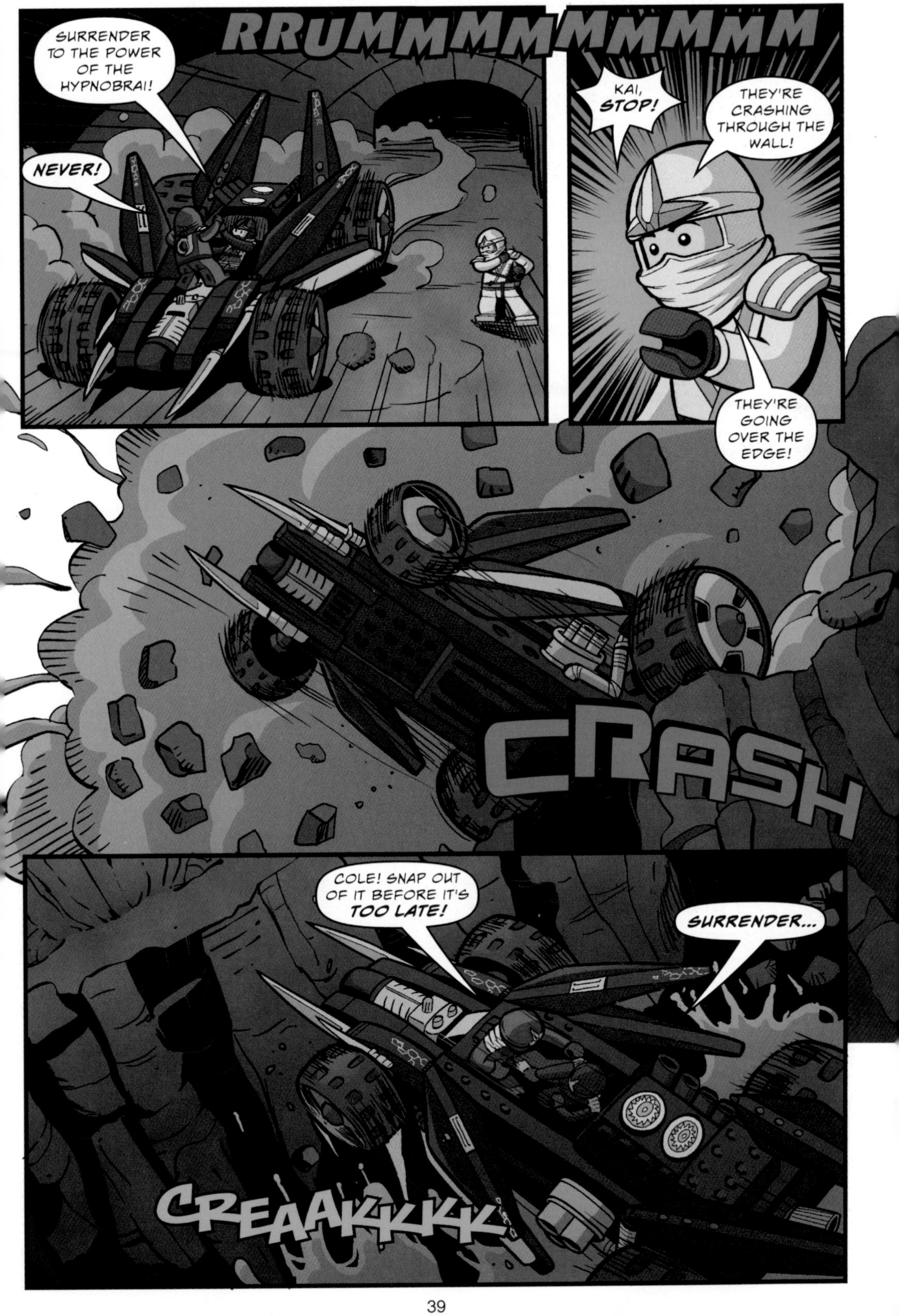
RRUMMMMMMMMMM
SURRENDER TO THE POWER OF THE HYPNOBRAI!
NEVER!
KAI, STOP!
THEY'RE CRASHING THROUGH THE WALL!
THEY'RE GOING OVER THE EDGE!
CRASH
COLE! SNAP OUT OF IT BEFORE IT'S TOO LATE!
SURRENDER...
CREAAKKKKK

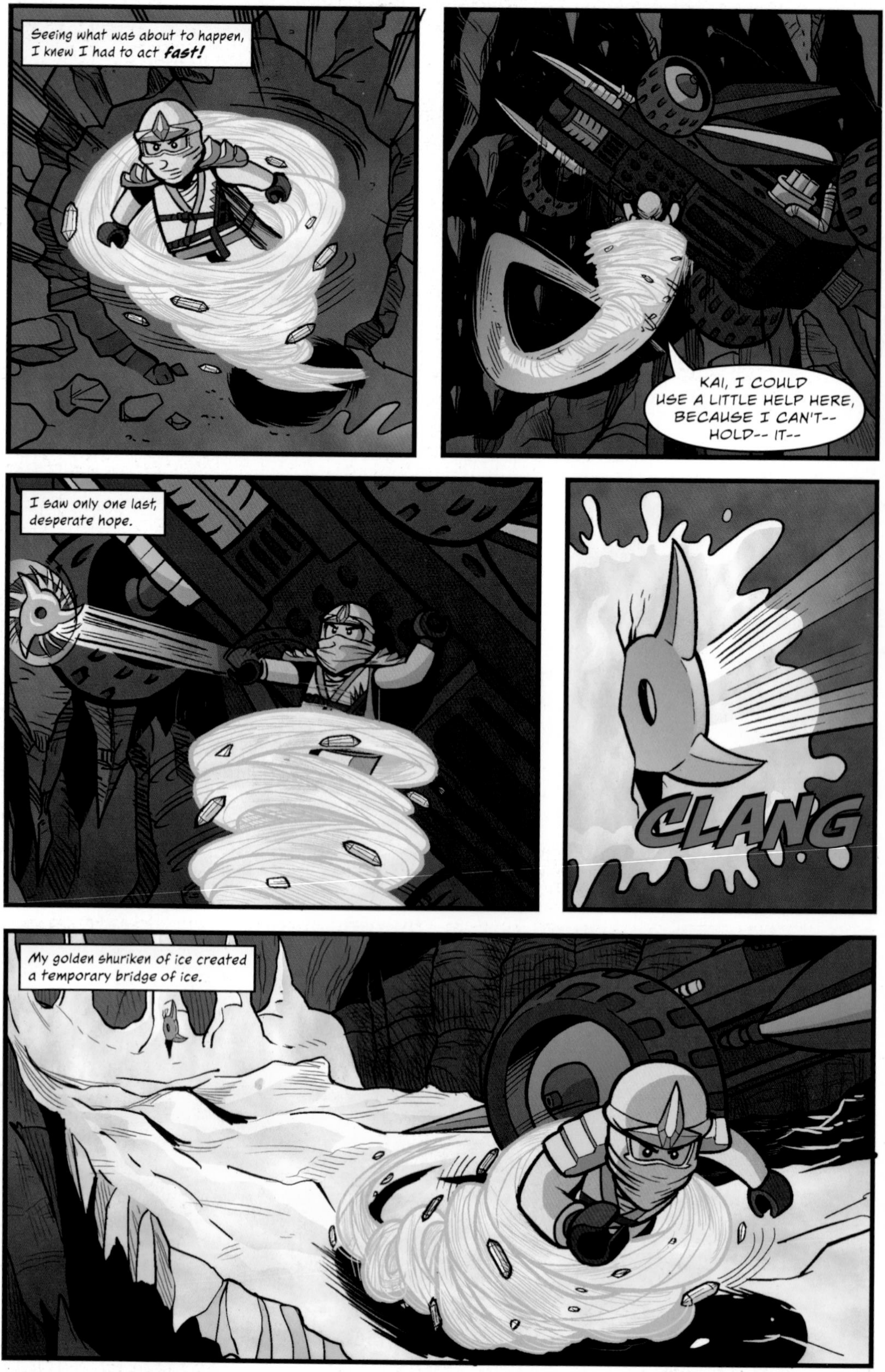
Seeing what was about to happen, I knew I had to act fast!
KAI, I COULD USE A LITTLE HELP HERE, BECAUSE I CAN'T-- HOLD-- IT--
I saw only one last, desperate hope.
CLANG
My golden shuriken of ice created a temporary bridge of ice.

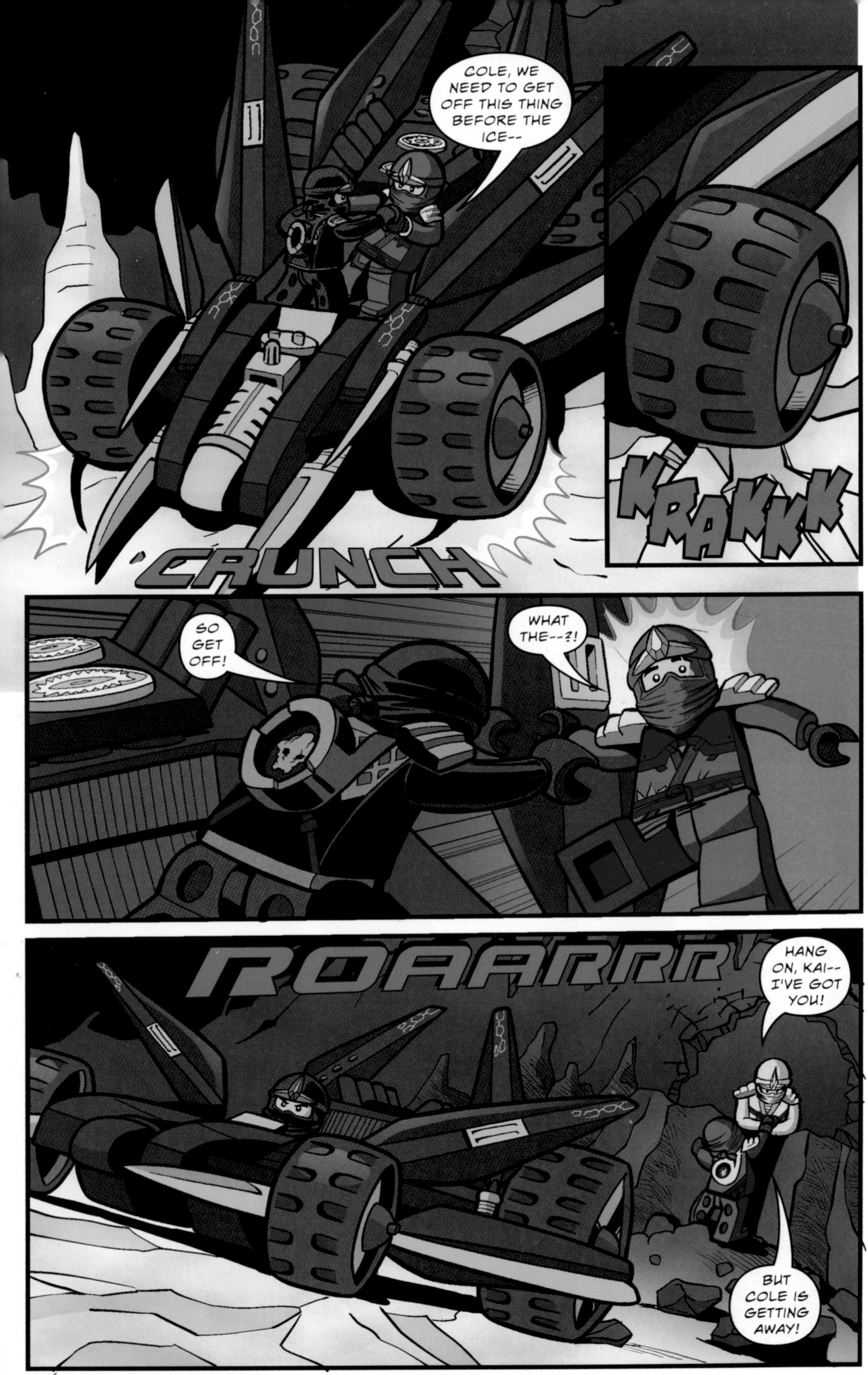
COLE, WE NEED TO GET OFF THIS THING BEFORE THE ICE--
CRUNCH
KRAKKK
SO GET OFF!
WHAT THE--?!
ROAARRR
HANG ON, KAI-- I'VE GOT YOU!
BUT COLE IS GETTING AWAY!

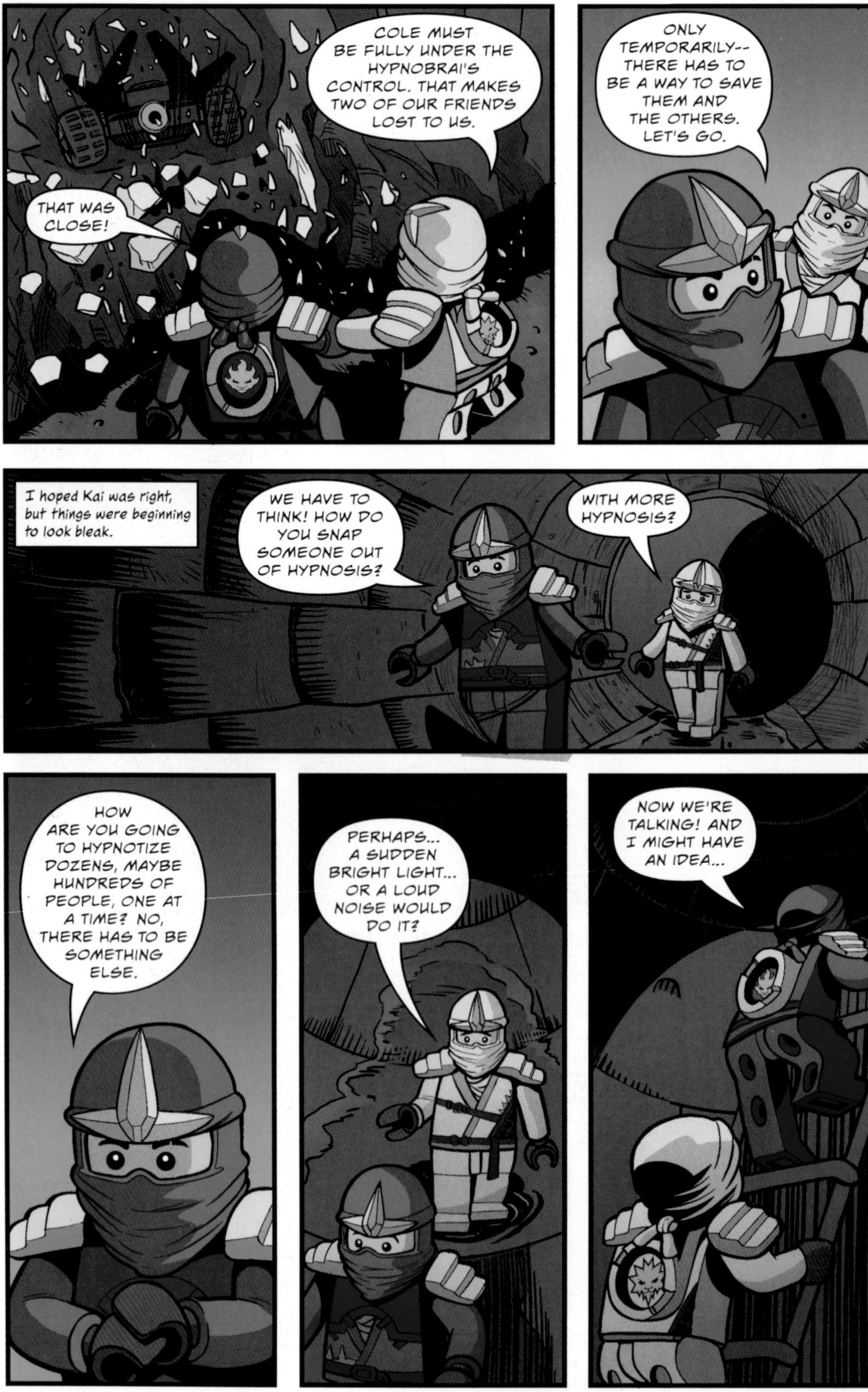
COLE MUST BE FULLY UNDER THE HYPNOBRAI'S CONTROL. THAT MAKES TWO OF OUR FRIENDS LOST TO US.
THAT WAS CLOSE!
ONLY TEMPORARILY-- THERE HAS TO BE A WAY TO SAVE THEM AND THE OTHERS. LET'S GO.
I hoped Kai was right, but things were beginning to look bleak.
WE HAVE TO THINK! HOW DO YOU SNAP SOMEONE OUT OF HYPNOSIS?
WITH MORE HYPNOSIS?
HOW ARE YOU GOING TO HYPNOTIZE DOZENS, MAYBE HUNDREDS OF PEOPLE, ONE AT A TIME? NO, THERE HAS TO BE SOMETHING ELSE.
PERHAPS... A SUDDEN BRIGHT LIGHT... OR A LOUD NOISE WOULD DO IT?
NOW WE'RE TALKING! AND I MIGHT HAVE AN IDEA...

Kai did not share his plan, insisting that we head for the warehouse the old man had mentioned. We stayed in the shadows, for obvious reasons...

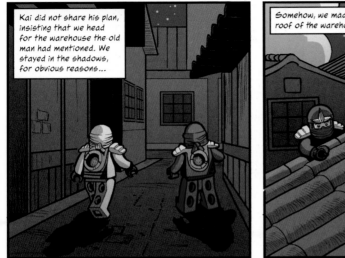

Somehow, we made it to the roof of the warehouse unseen...

Finding a skylight, we peered down at an amazing sight...

The warehouse had been converted into a vehicle factory for the Hypnobrai!

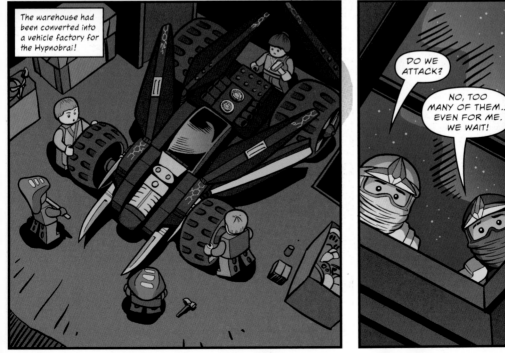

DO WE ATTACK?

NO, TOO MANY OF THEM... EVEN FOR ME. WE WAIT!

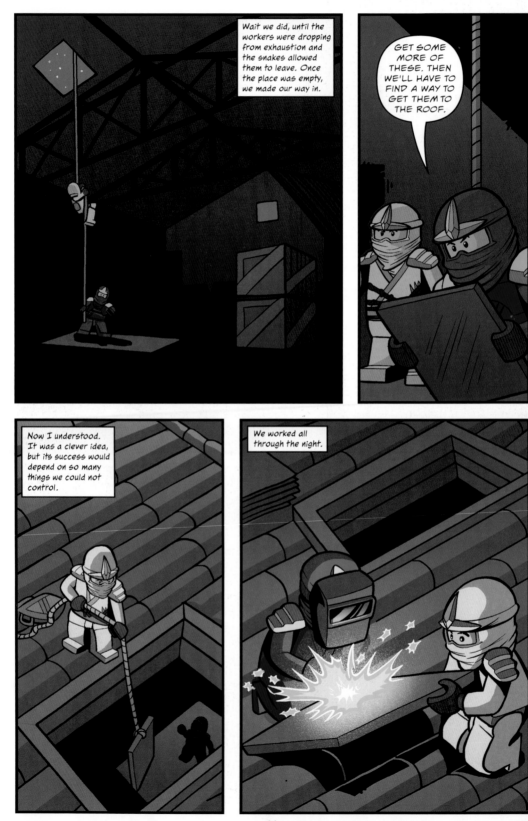

Wait we did, until the workers were dropping from exhaustion and the snakes allowed them to leave. Once the place was empty, we made our way in.

GET SOME MORE OF THESE. THEN WE'LL HAVE TO FIND A WAY TO GET THEM TO THE ROOF.

Now I understood. It was a clever idea, but its success would depend on so many things we could not control.

We worked all through the night.

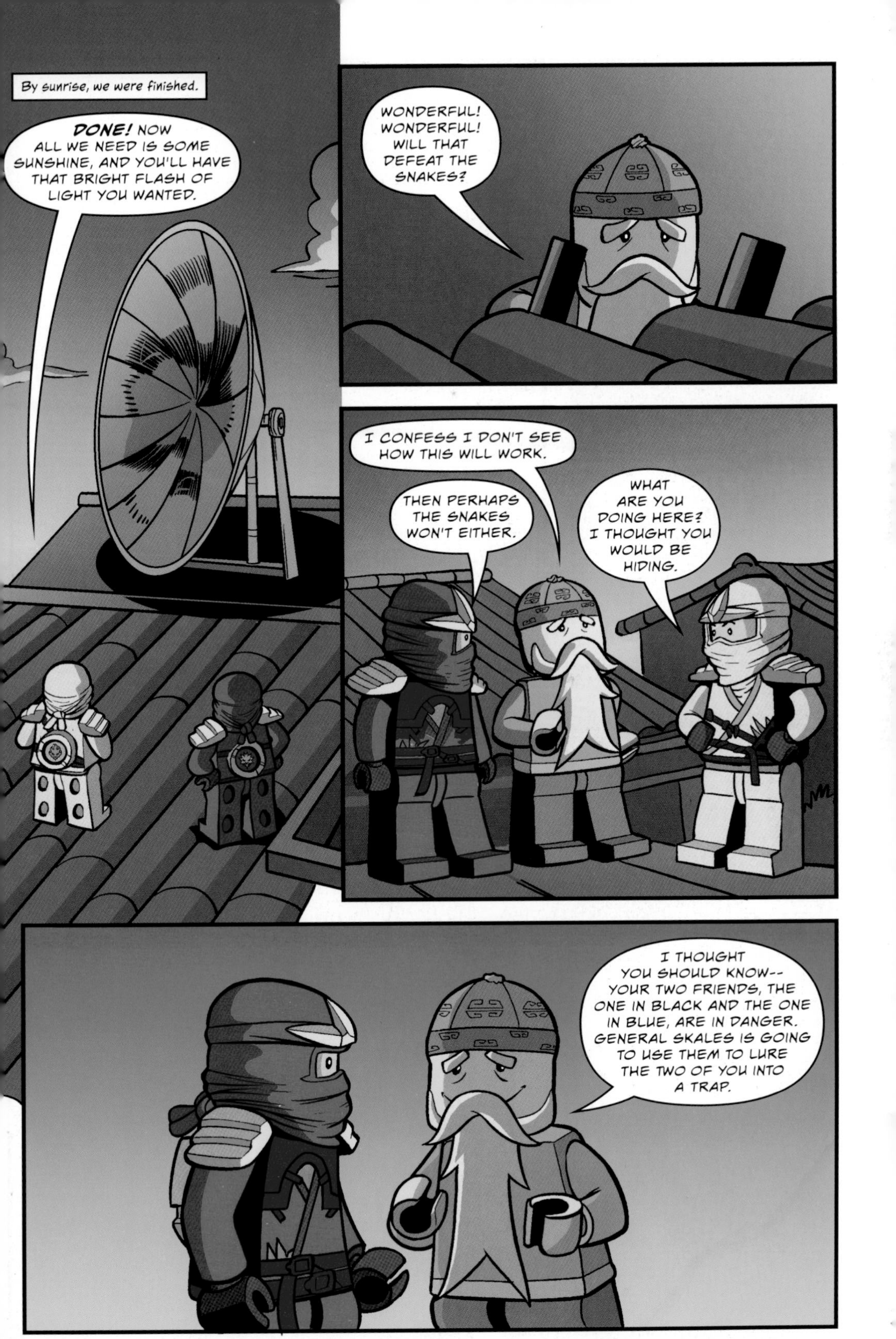
By sunrise, we were finished.
DONE! NOW ALL WE NEED IS SOME SUNSHINE, AND YOU'LL HAVE THAT BRIGHT FLASH OF LIGHT YOU WANTED.
WONDERFUL! WONDERFUL! WILL THAT DEFEAT THE SNAKES?
I CONFESS I DON'T SEE HOW THIS WILL WORK.
THEN PERHAPS THE SNAKES WON'T EITHER.
WHAT ARE YOU DOING HERE? I THOUGHT YOU WOULD BE HIDING.
I THOUGHT YOU SHOULD KNOW-- YOUR TWO FRIENDS, THE ONE IN BLACK AND THE ONE IN BLUE, ARE IN DANGER. GENERAL SKALES IS GOING TO USE THEM TO LURE THE TWO OF YOU INTO A TRAP.

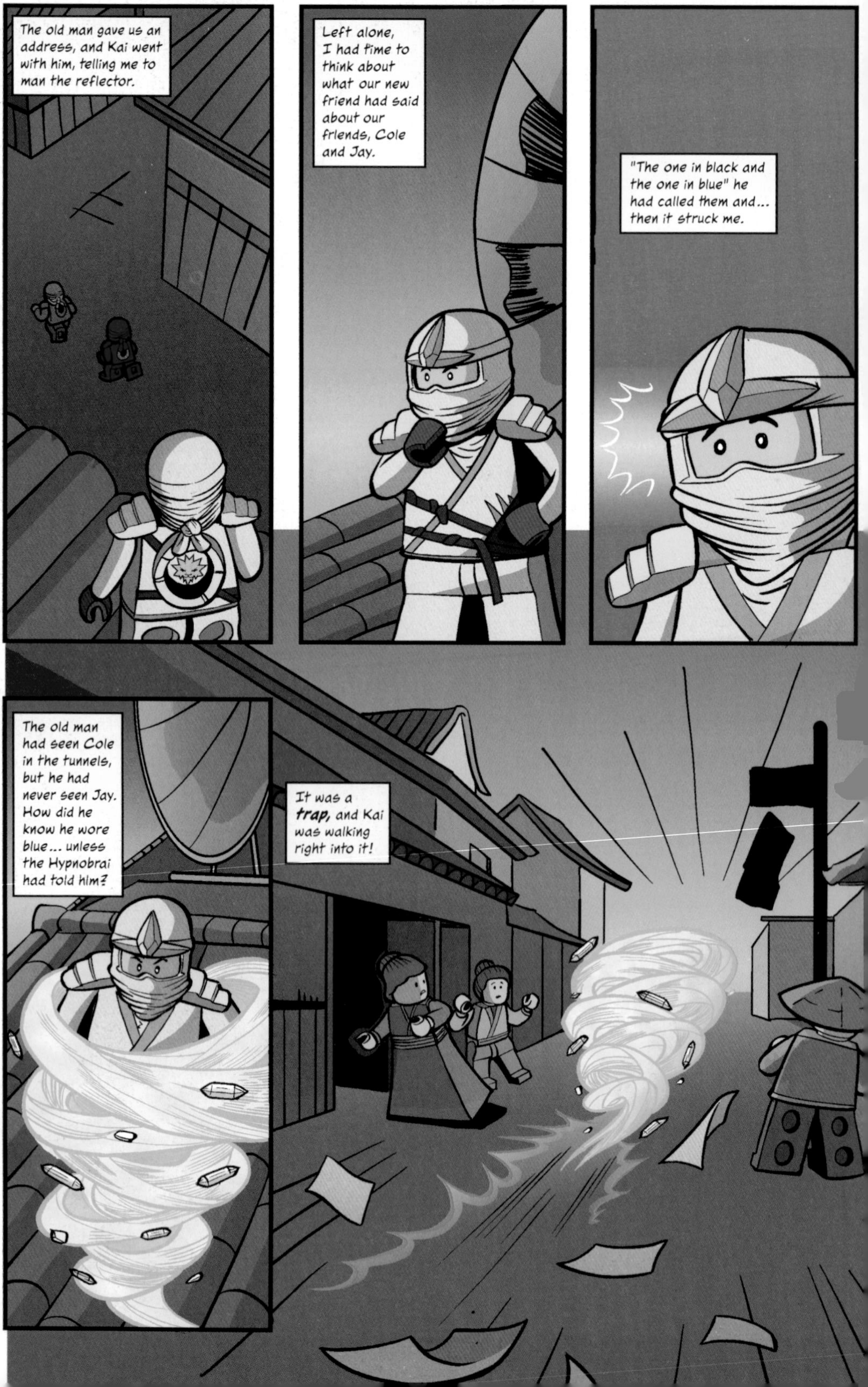

The old man gave us an address, and Kai went with him, telling me to man the reflector.
Left alone, I had time to think about what our new friend had said about our friends, Cole and Jay.
"The one in black and the one in blue" he had called them and... then it struck me.
The old man had seen Cole in the tunnels, but he had never seen Jay. How did he know he wore blue... unless the Hypnobrai had told him?
It was a ***trap,*** and Kai was walking right into it!

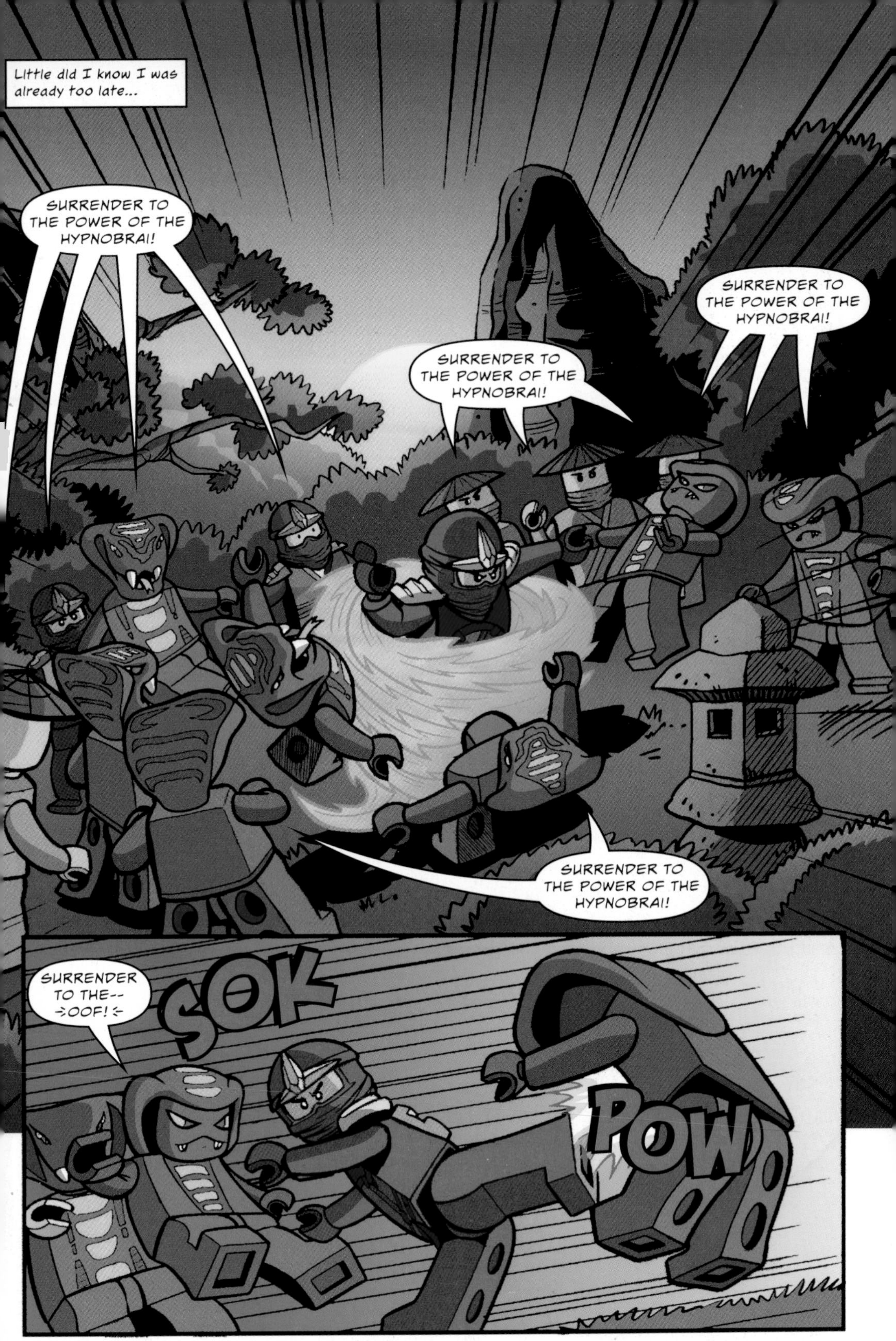
Little did I know I was already too late...
SURRENDER TO THE POWER OF THE HYPNOBRAI!
SURRENDER TO THE POWER OF THE HYPNOBRAI!
SURRENDER TO THE POWER OF THE HYPNOBRAI!
SURRENDER TO THE POWER OF THE HYPNOBRAI!
SURRENDER TO THE-- OOF!
SOK
POW

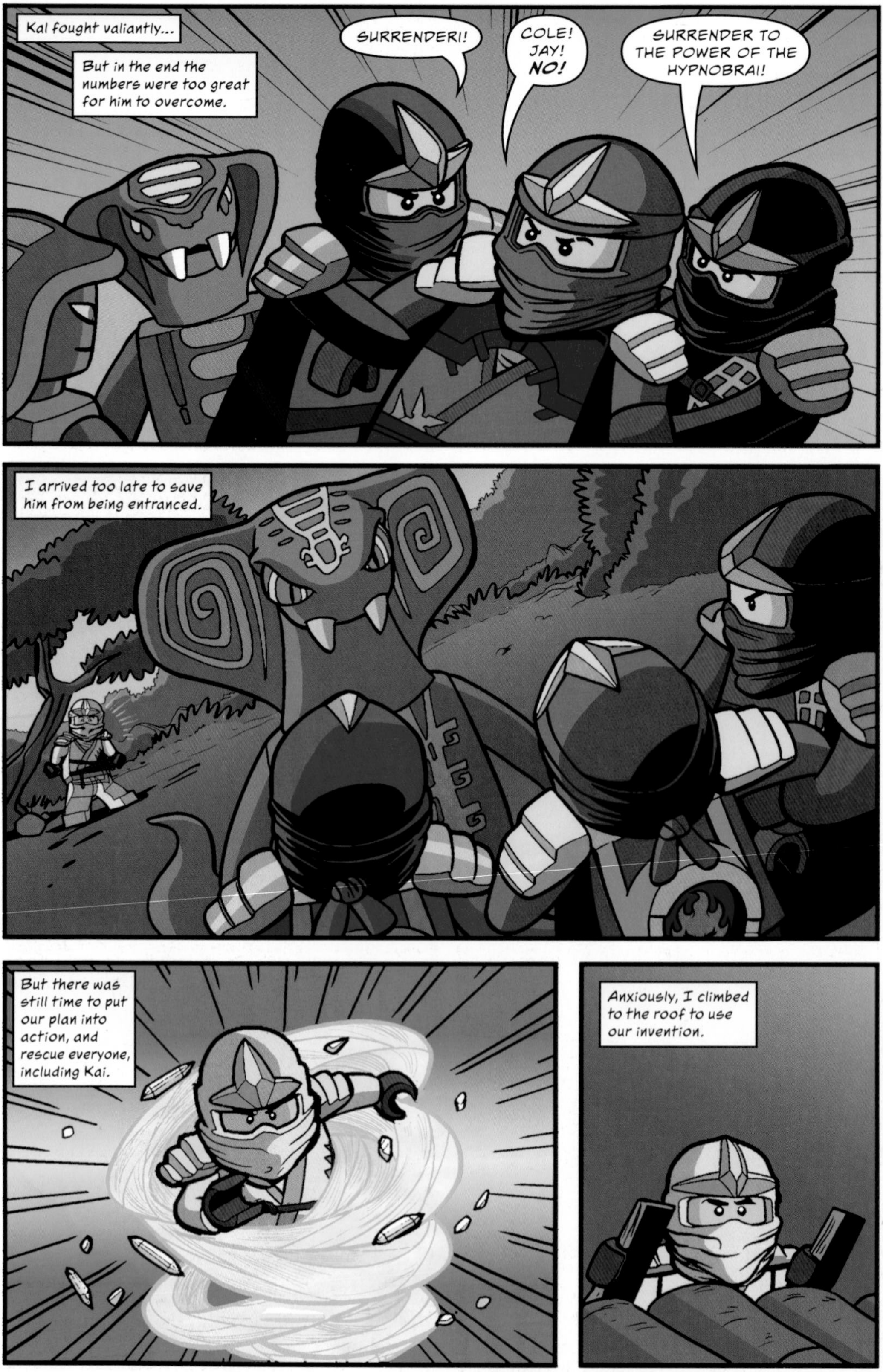
Kal fought valiantly...
But in the end the numbers were too great for him to overcome.
SURRENDER!!
COLE! JAY! **NO!**
SURRENDER TO THE POWER OF THE HYPNOBRAI!
I arrived too late to save him from being entranced.
But there was still time to put our plan into action, and rescue everyone, including Kai.
Anxiously, I climbed to the roof to use our invention.

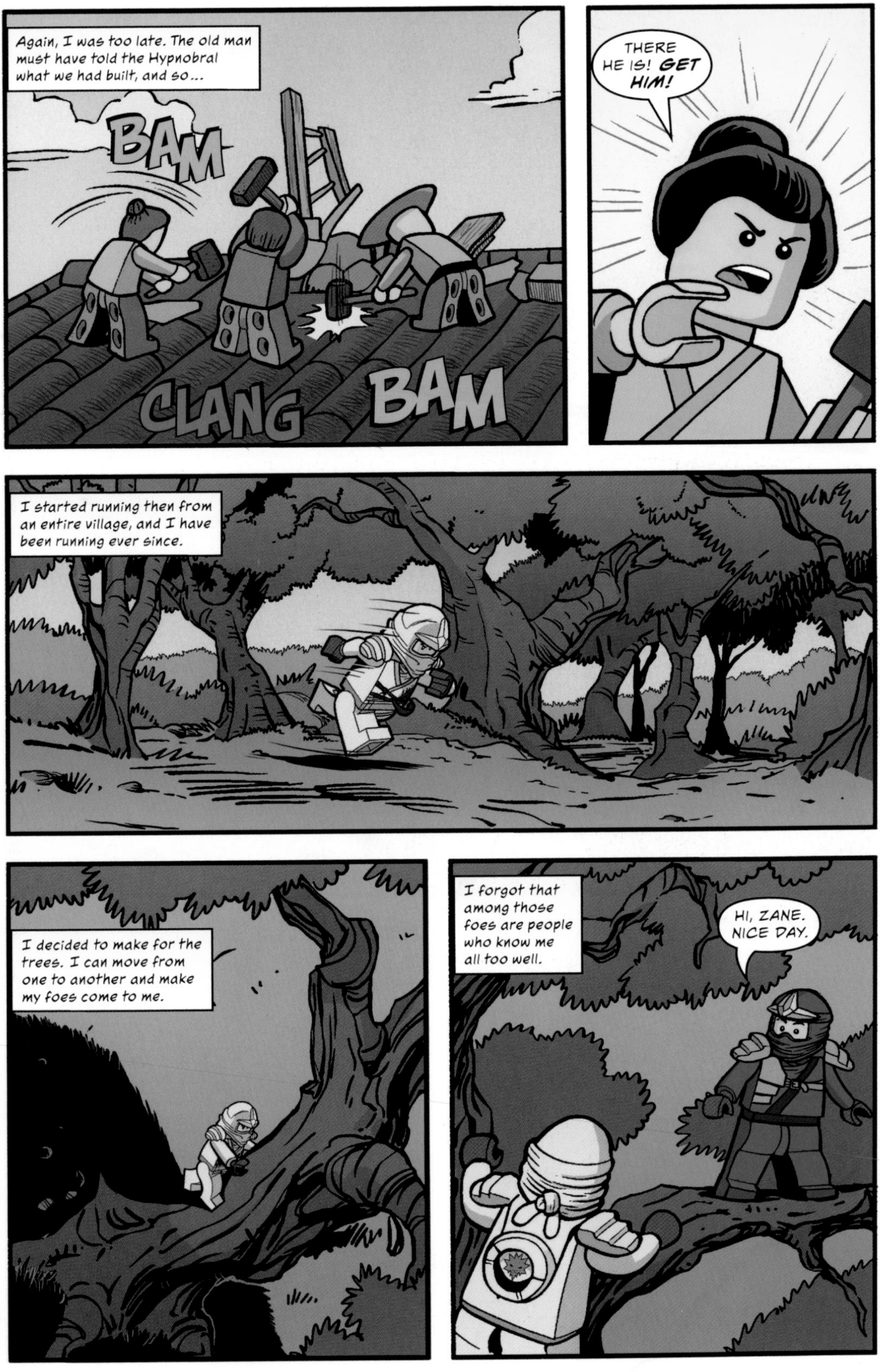
Again, I was too late. The old man must have told the Hypnobral what we had built, and so...
BAM
CLANG
BAM
THERE HE IS! GET HIM!
I started running then from an entire village, and I have been running ever since.
I decided to make for the trees. I can move from one to another and make my foes come to me.
I forgot that among those foes are people who know me all too well.
HI, ZANE. NICE DAY.

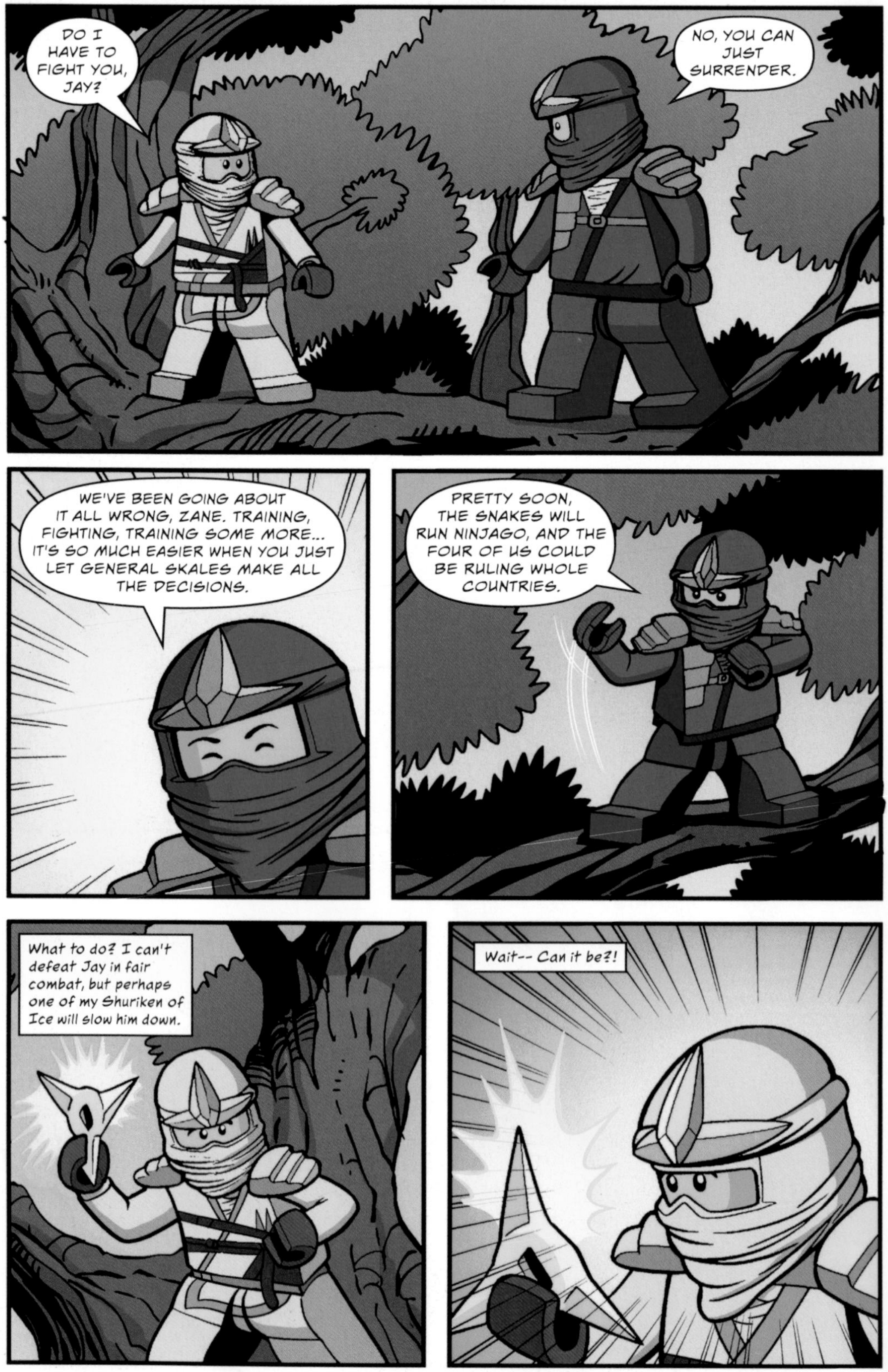
DO I HAVE TO FIGHT YOU, JAY?
NO, YOU CAN JUST SURRENDER.
WE'VE BEEN GOING ABOUT IT ALL WRONG, ZANE. TRAINING, FIGHTING, TRAINING SOME MORE... IT'S SO MUCH EASIER WHEN YOU JUST LET GENERAL SKALES MAKE ALL THE DECISIONS.
PRETTY SOON, THE SNAKES WILL RUN NINJAGO, AND THE FOUR OF US COULD BE RULING WHOLE COUNTRIES.
What to do? I can't defeat Jay in fair combat, but perhaps one of my Shuriken of Ice will slow him down.
Wait-- Can it be?!

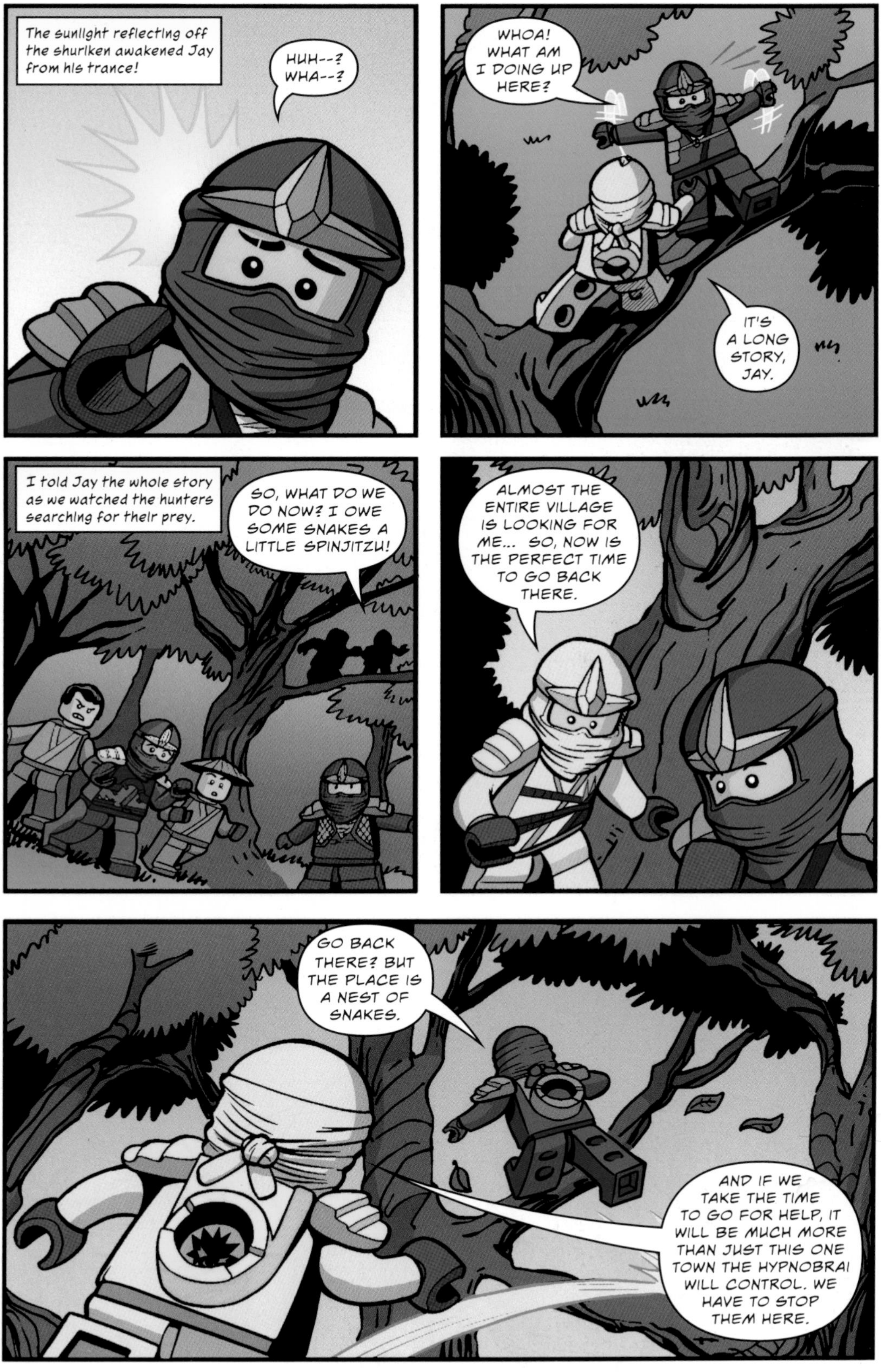

The sunlight reflecting off the shuriken awakened Jay from his trance!
HUH--? WHA--?
WHOA! WHAT AM I DOING UP HERE?
IT'S A LONG STORY, JAY.
I told Jay the whole story as we watched the hunters searching for their prey.
SO, WHAT DO WE DO NOW? I OWE SOME SNAKES A LITTLE SPINJITZU!
ALMOST THE ENTIRE VILLAGE IS LOOKING FOR ME... SO, NOW IS THE PERFECT TIME TO GO BACK THERE.
GO BACK THERE? BUT THE PLACE IS A NEST OF SNAKES.
AND IF WE TAKE THE TIME TO GO FOR HELP, IT WILL BE MUCH MORE THAN JUST THIS ONE TOWN THE HYPNOBRAI WILL CONTROL. WE HAVE TO STOP THEM HERE.

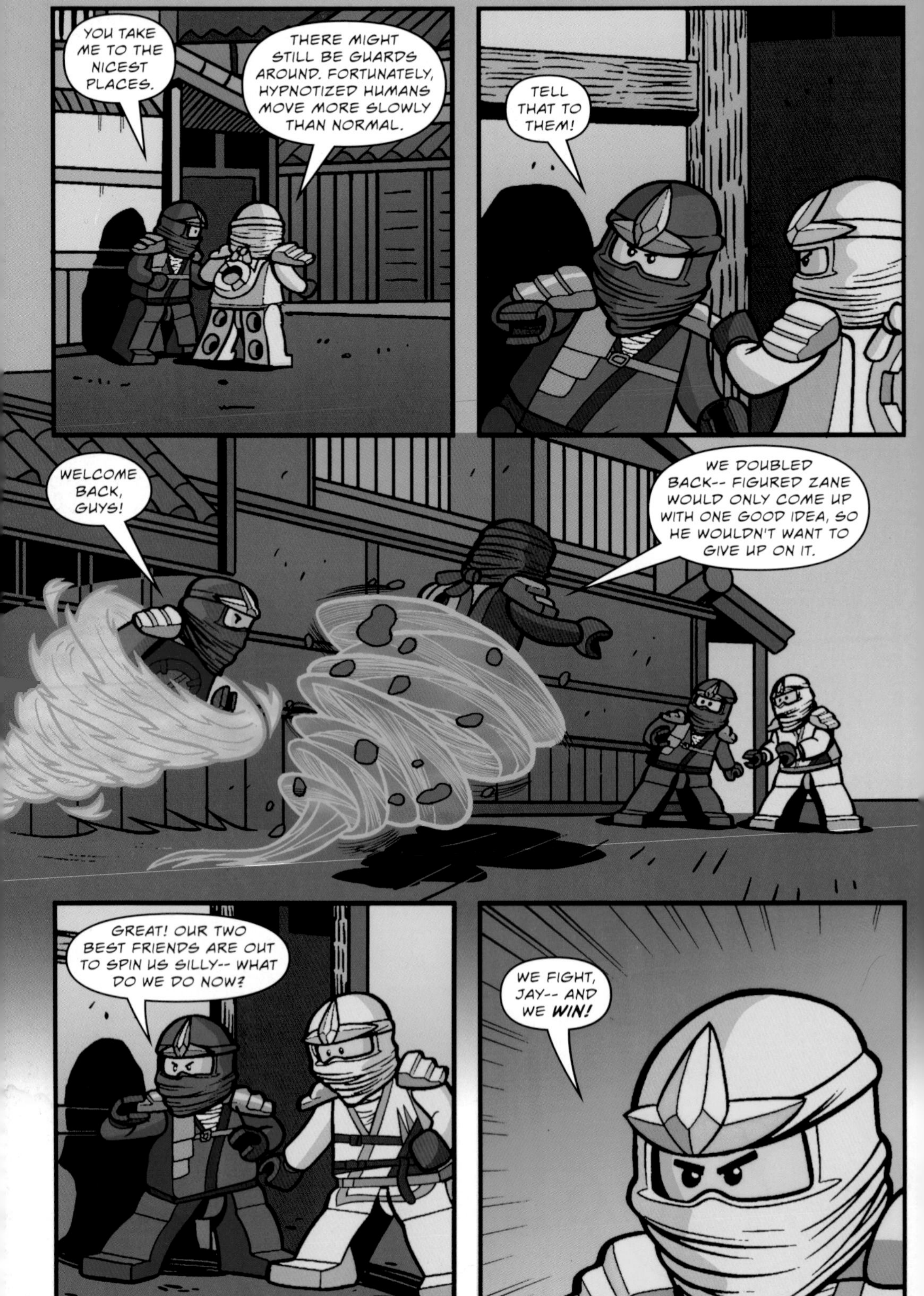
YOU TAKE ME TO THE NICEST PLACES.
THERE MIGHT STILL BE GUARDS AROUND. FORTUNATELY, HYPNOTIZED HUMANS MOVE MORE SLOWLY THAN NORMAL.
TELL THAT TO THEM!
WELCOME BACK, GUYS!
WE DOUBLED BACK-- FIGURED ZANE WOULD ONLY COME UP WITH ONE GOOD IDEA, SO HE WOULDN'T WANT TO GIVE UP ON IT.
GREAT! OUR TWO BEST FRIENDS ARE OUT TO SPIN US SILLY-- WHAT DO WE DO NOW?
WE FIGHT, JAY-- AND WE **WIN!**

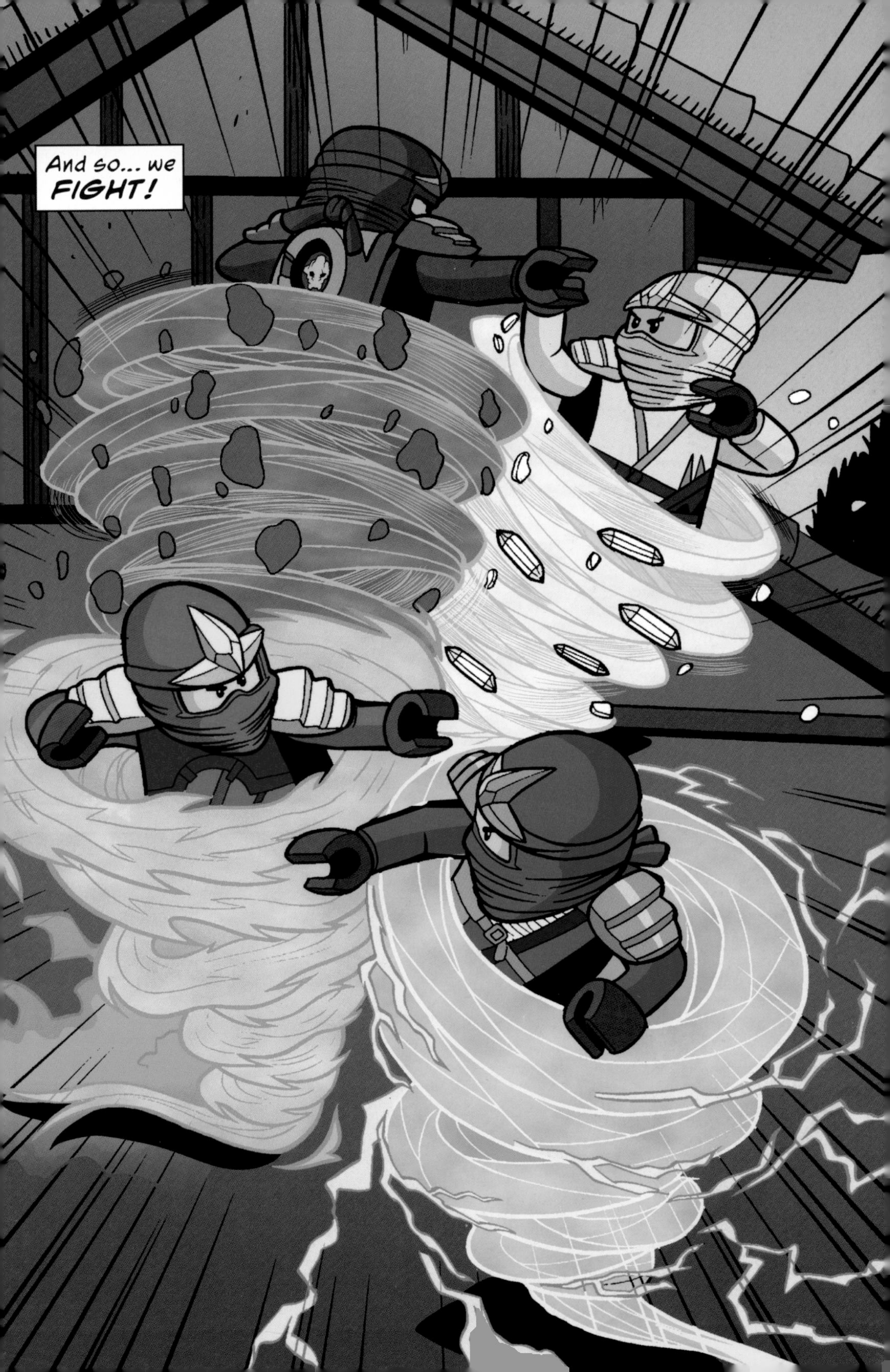
And so... we FIGHT!

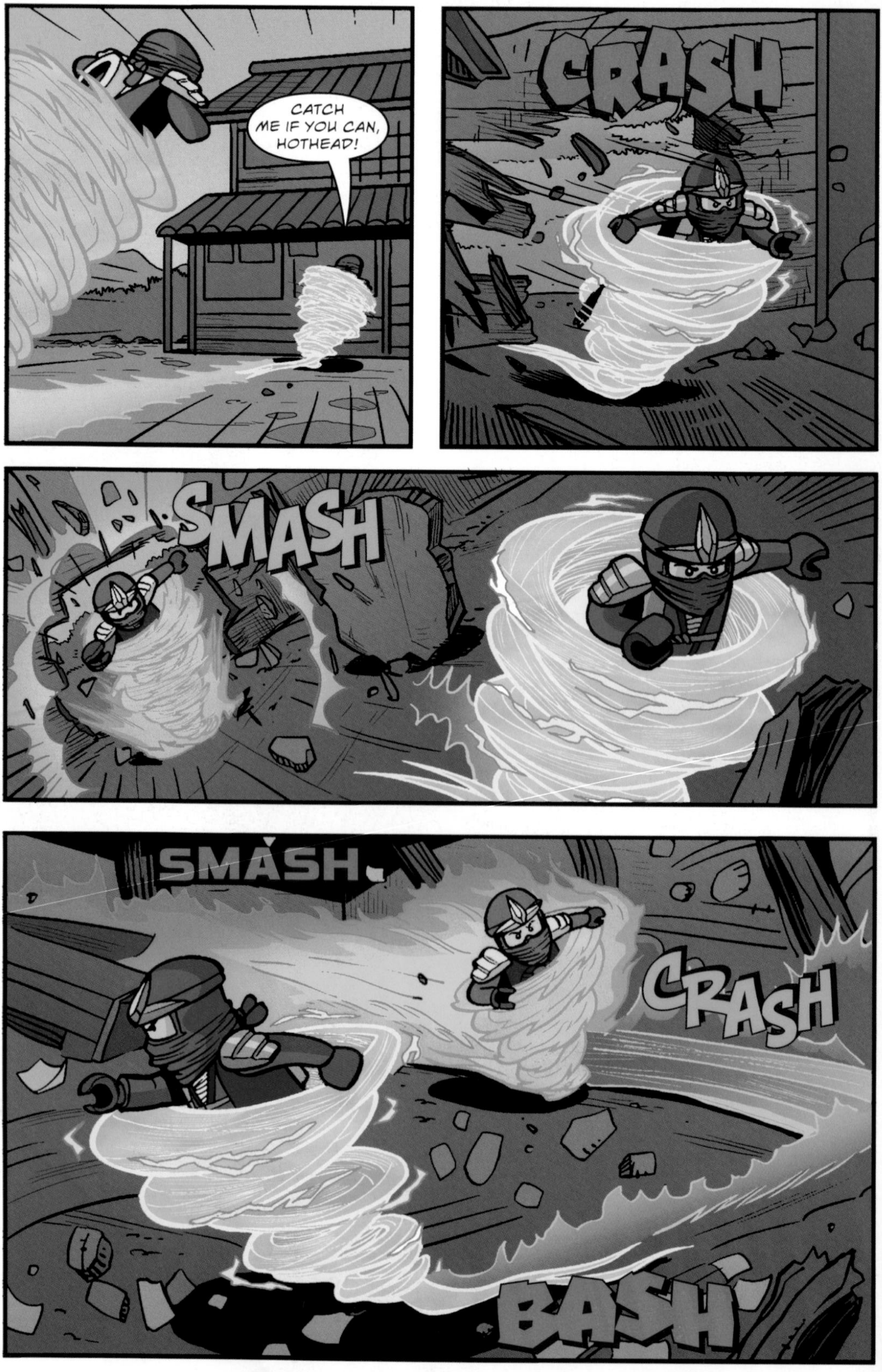
CATCH ME IF YOU CAN, HOTHEAD!
CRASH
SMASH
SMASH
CRASH
BASH

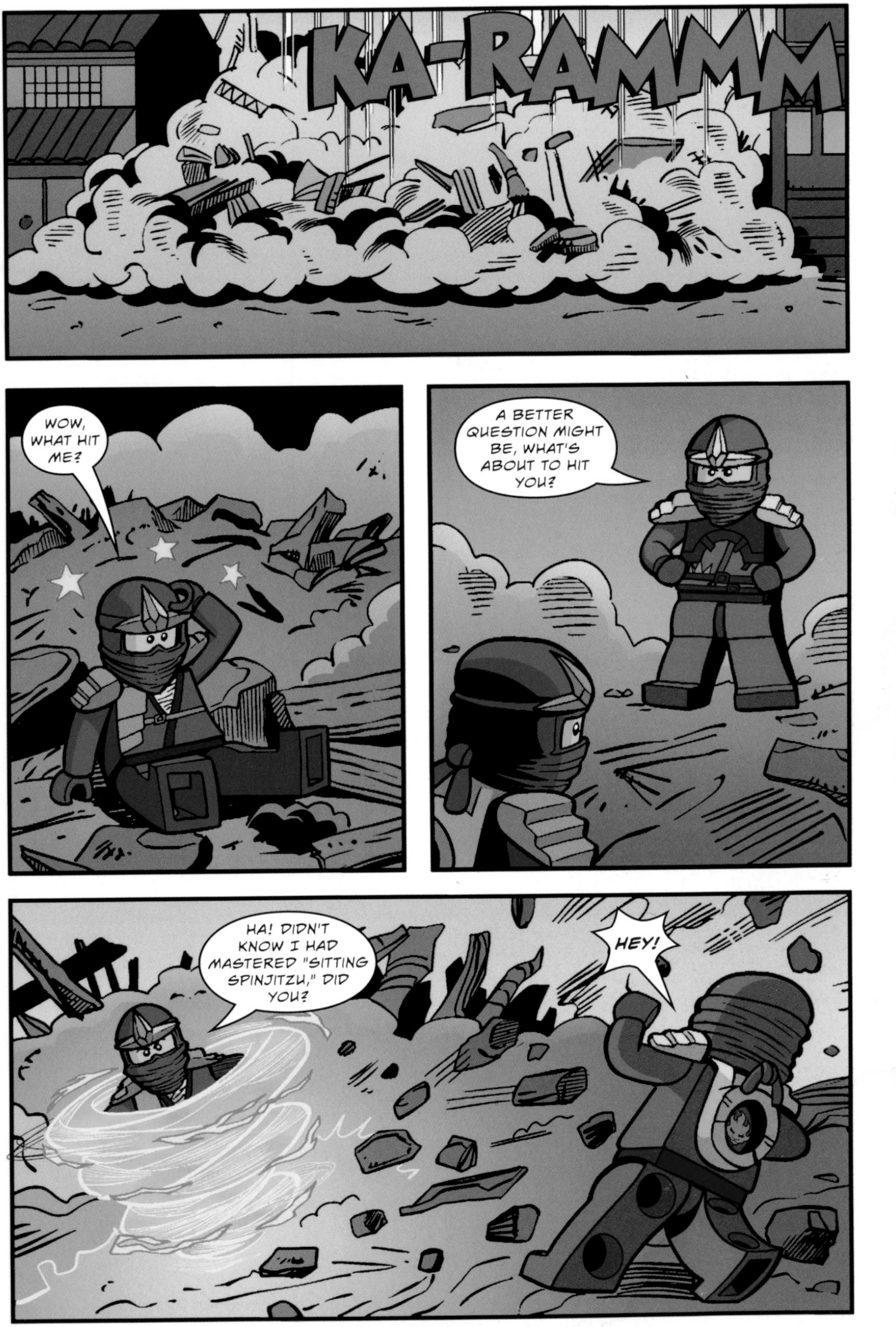
KA-RAMMM
WOW, WHAT HIT ME?
A BETTER QUESTION MIGHT BE, WHAT'S ABOUT TO HIT YOU?
HA! DIDN'T KNOW I HAD MASTERED "SITTING SPINJITZU," DID YOU?
HEY!

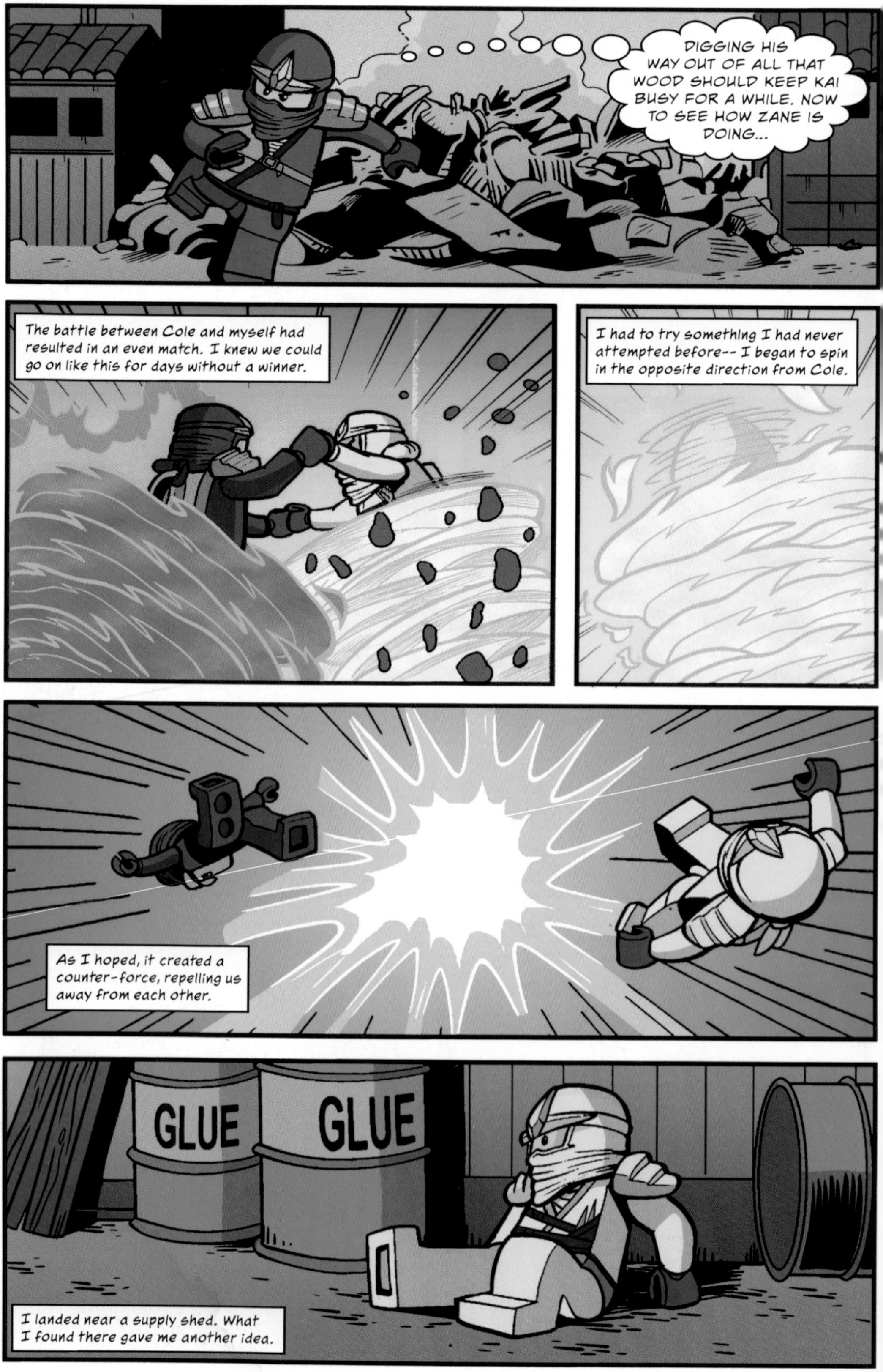
DIGGING HIS WAY OUT OF ALL THAT WOOD SHOULD KEEP KAI BUSY FOR A WHILE. NOW TO SEE HOW ZANE IS DOING...
The battle between Cole and myself had resulted in an even match. I knew we could go on like this for days without a winner.
I had to try something I had never attempted before-- I began to spin in the opposite direction from Cole.
As I hoped, it created a counter-force, repelling us away from each other.
GLUE
GLUE
I landed near a supply shed. What I found there gave me another idea.

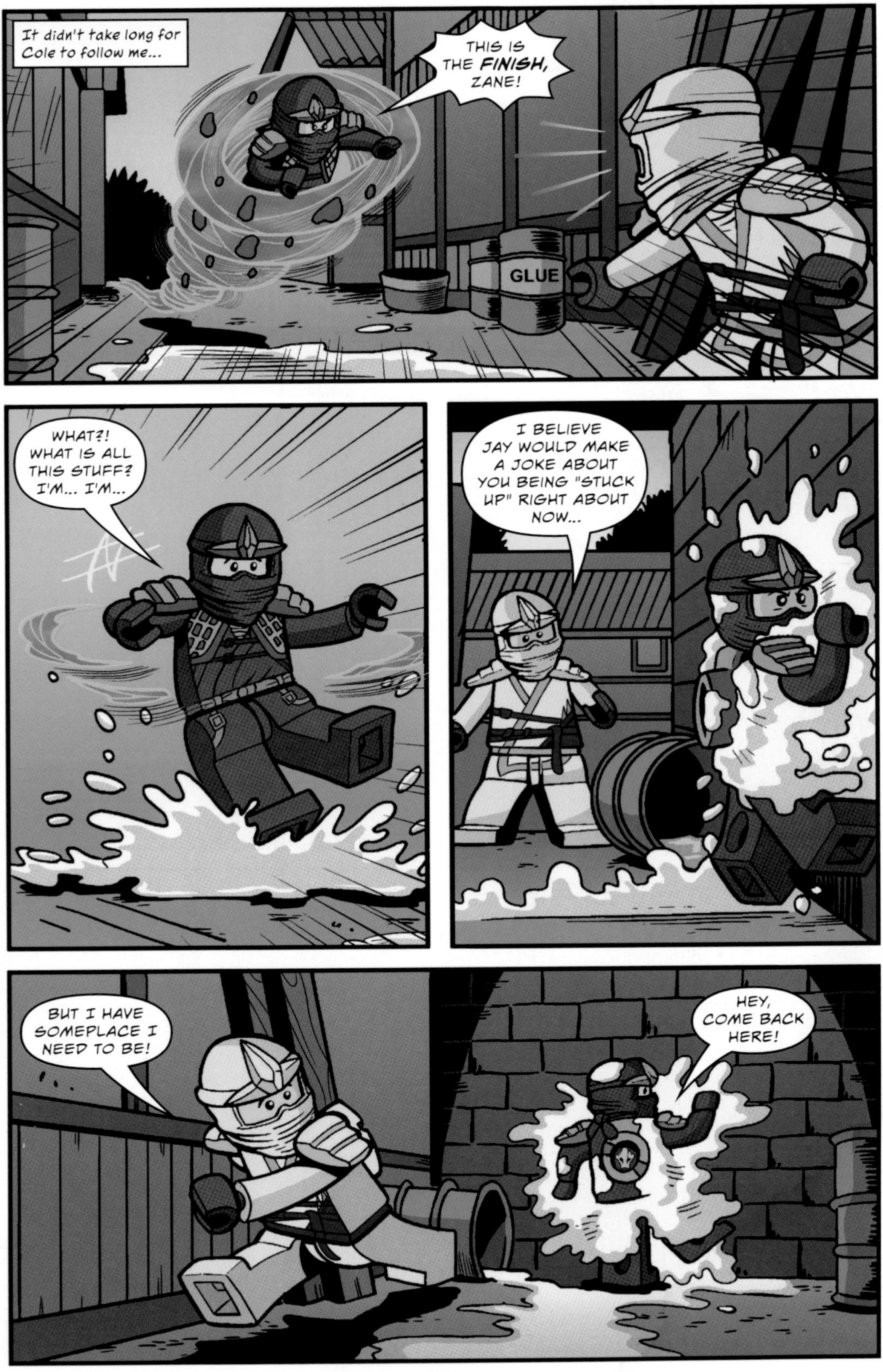

It didn't take long for Cole to follow me...
THIS IS THE FINISH, ZANE!
GLUE
WHAT?! WHAT IS ALL THIS STUFF? I'M... I'M...
I BELIEVE JAY WOULD MAKE A JOKE ABOUT YOU BEING "STUCK UP" RIGHT ABOUT NOW...
BUT I HAVE SOMEPLACE I NEED TO BE!
HEY, COME BACK HERE!

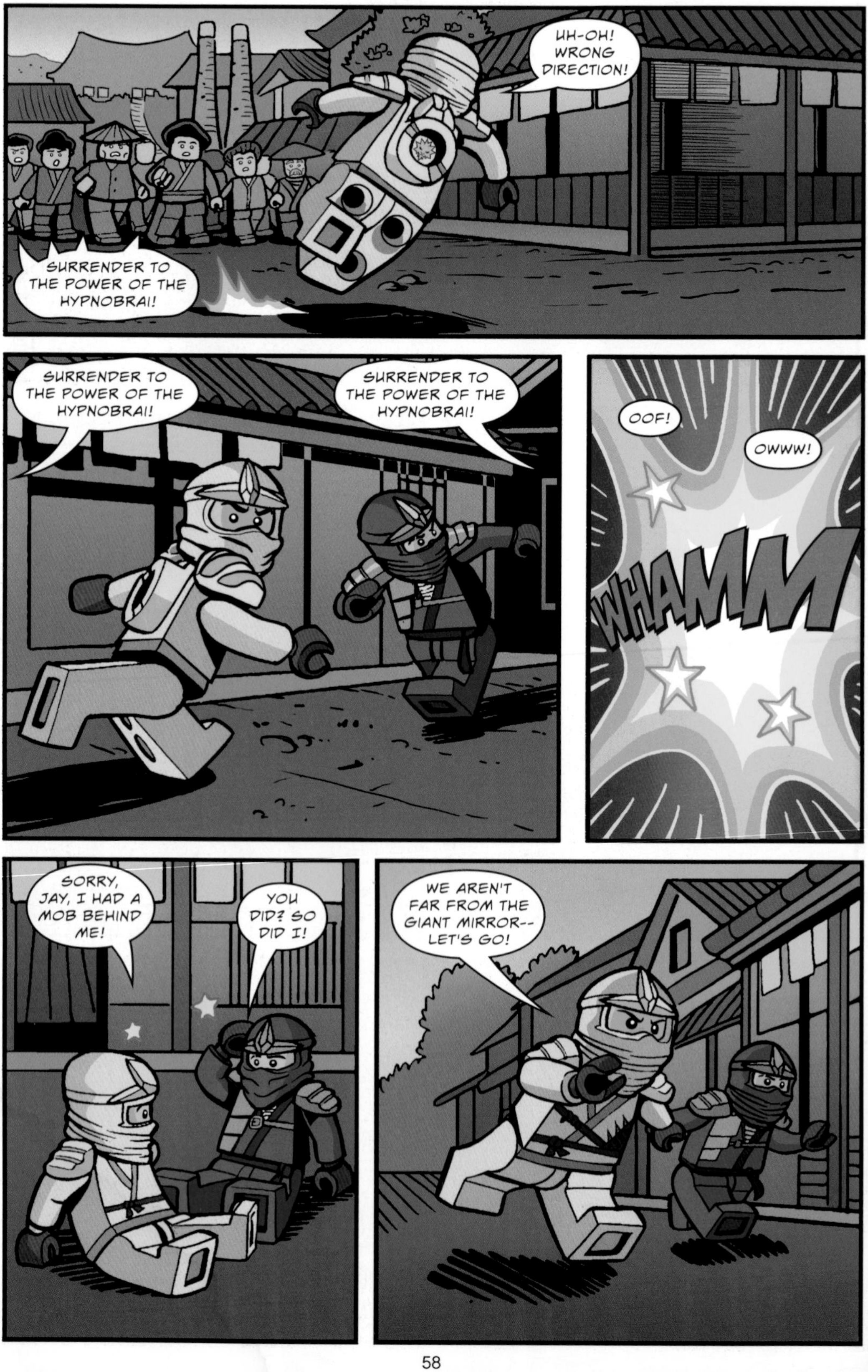
UH-OH! WRONG DIRECTION!
SURRENDER TO THE POWER OF THE HYPNOBRAI!
SURRENDER TO THE POWER OF THE HYPNOBRAI!
SURRENDER TO THE POWER OF THE HYPNOBRAI!
OOF!
OWWW!
WHAMM
SORRY, JAY, I HAD A MOB BEHIND ME!
YOU DID? SO DID I!
WE AREN'T FAR FROM THE GIANT MIRROR-- LET'S GO!

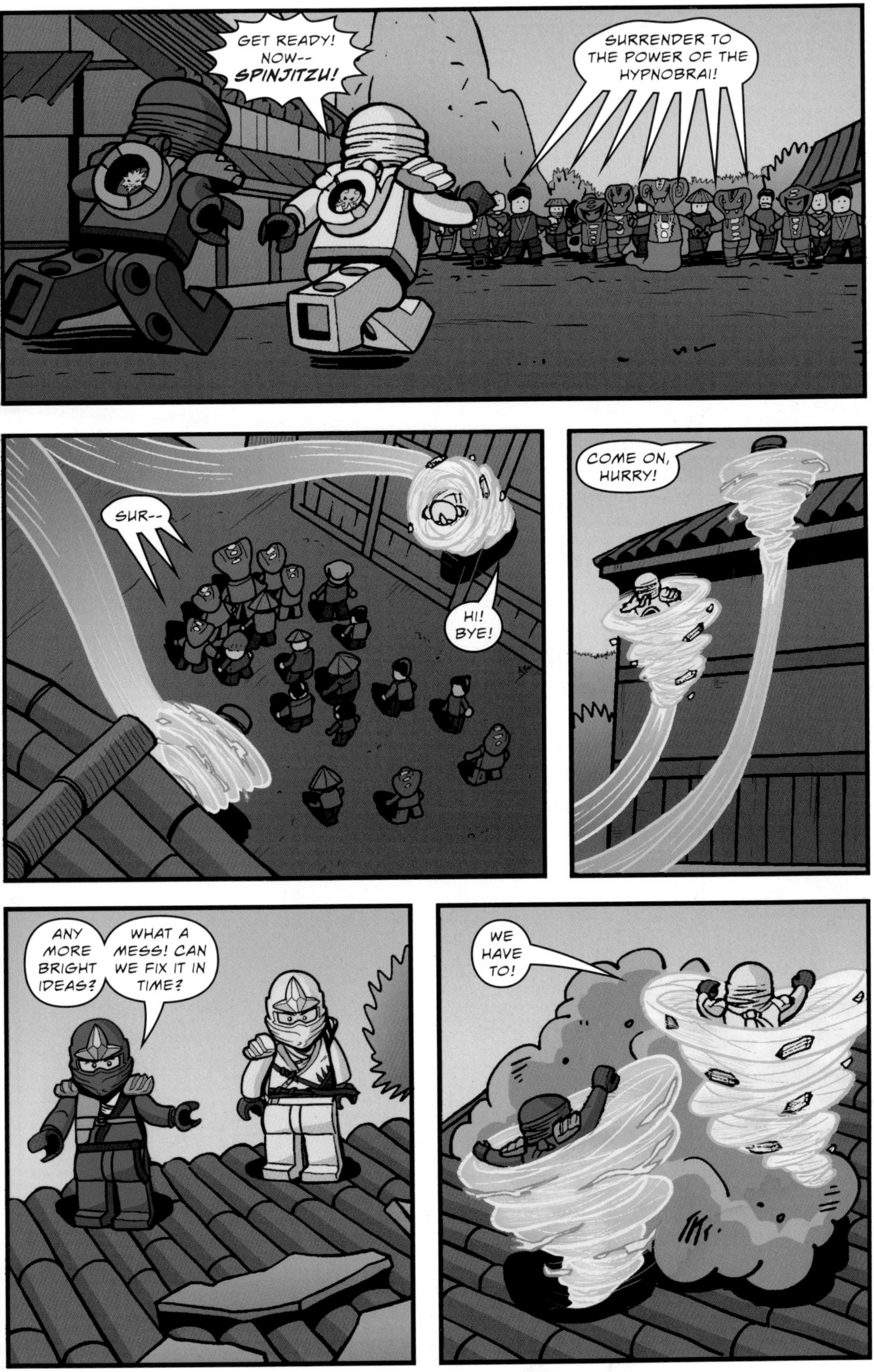
GET READY! NOW-- **SPINJITZU!**
SURRENDER TO THE POWER OF THE HYPNOBRAI!
SUR--
HI! BYE!
COME ON, HURRY!
ANY MORE BRIGHT IDEAS?
WHAT A MESS! CAN WE FIX IT IN TIME?
WE HAVE TO!

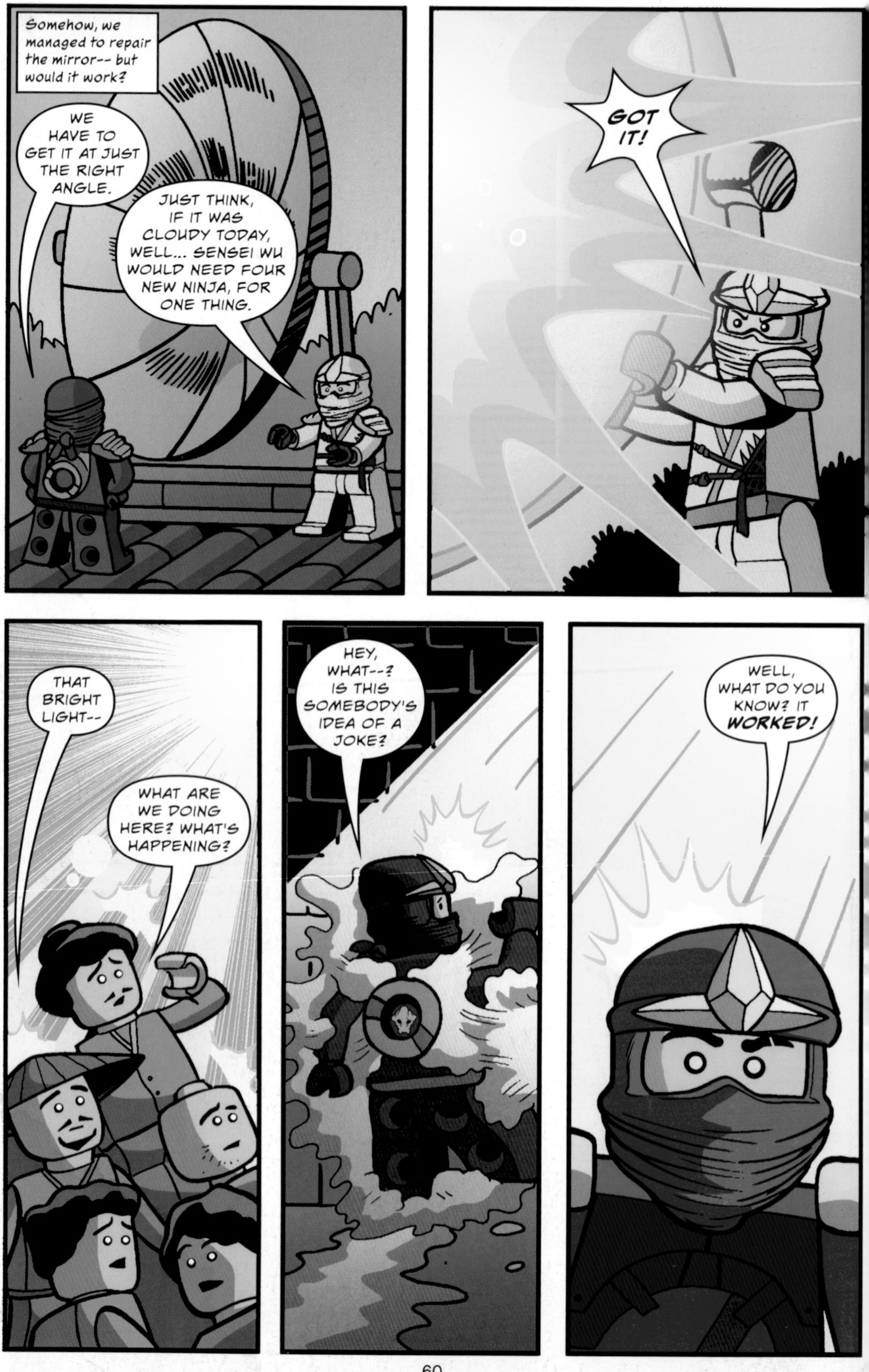

Somehow, we managed to repair the mirror-- but would it work?
WE HAVE TO GET IT AT JUST THE RIGHT ANGLE.
JUST THINK, IF IT WAS CLOUDY TODAY, WELL... SENSEI WU WOULD NEED FOUR NEW NINJA, FOR ONE THING.
GOT IT!
THAT BRIGHT LIGHT--
WHAT ARE WE DOING HERE? WHAT'S HAPPENING?
HEY, WHAT--? IS THIS SOMEBODY'S IDEA OF A JOKE?
WELL, WHAT DO YOU KNOW? IT **WORKED!**

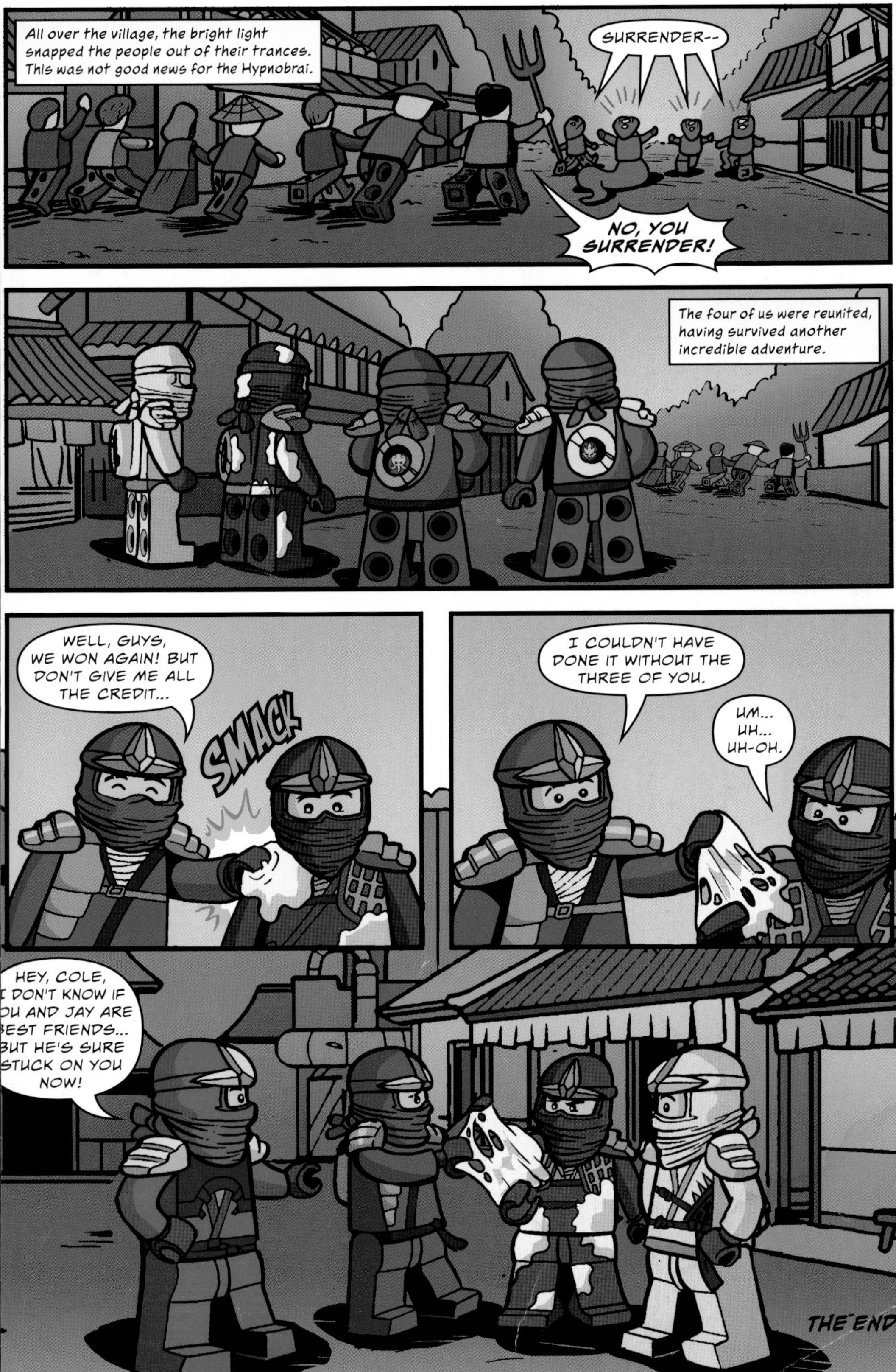
All over the village, the bright light snapped the people out of their trances. This was not good news for the Hypnobrai.
SURRENDER--
NO, YOU SURRENDER!
The four of us were reunited, having survived another incredible adventure.
WELL, GUYS, WE WON AGAIN! BUT DON'T GIVE ME ALL THE CREDIT...
SMACK
I COULDN'T HAVE DONE IT WITHOUT THE THREE OF YOU.
UM... UH... UH-OH.
HEY, COLE, I DON'T KNOW IF YOU AND JAY ARE BEST FRIENDS... BUT HE'S SURE STUCK ON YOU NOW!
THE END

the SMURFS™

GRAPHIC NOVELS AVAILABLE AT BOOKSELLERS EVERYWHERE AND DIGITALLY FROM COMIXOLOGY.COM...

THE PURPLE SMURFS
PAPERCUTZ

Graphic Novel #1

THE SMURFS AND THE MAGIC FLUTE
PAPERCUTZ

Graphic Novel #2

THE SMURF KING
PAPERCUTZ

Graphic Novel #3

THE SMURFETTE
PAPERCUTZ

Graphic Novel #4

THE SMURFS AND THE EGG
PAPERCUTZ

Graphic Novel #5

THE SMURFS AND THE HOWLIBIRD
PAPERCUTZ

Graphic Novel #6

THE ASTRO SMURF
PAPERCUTZ

Graphic Novel #7

THE SMURF APPRENTICE
PAPERCUTZ

Graphic Novel #8

GARGAMEL AND THE SMURFS
PAPERCUTZ

Graphic Novel #9

EACH GRAPHIC NOVEL IS 100% SMURFY!

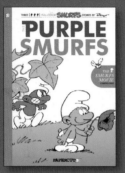

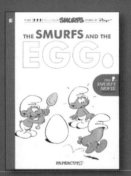

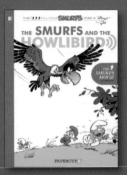

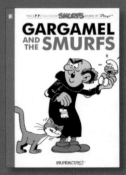

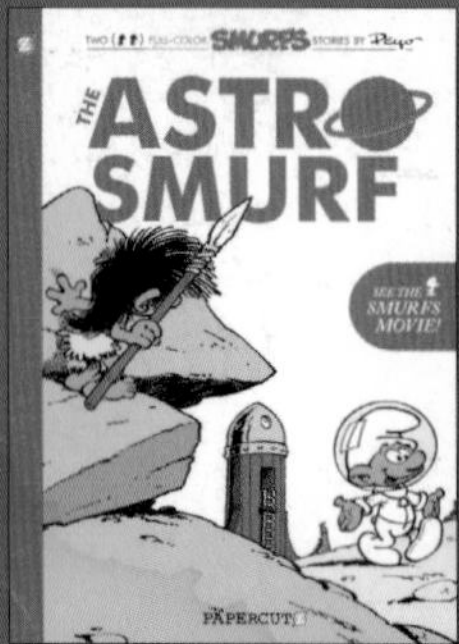

WATCH OUT FOR PAPERCUTZ

Surrender to the power of the Hypnobrai, Michael Petranek! Everyone must surrender to the power of the Hypnobrai! You belong at the factory, on the assembly line! Surrender to the power of the Hypnobrai! What is that object in your hand, Michael Petranek? It is very BRIGHT--!

Yow! Oh, my goodness! I been hypnotized! Thanks to my trusty, hard-working Associate Editor, and his shiny cellphone, I'm back to normal. Or as close to normal as I ever get! That was really weird -- Michael tells me my eyes looked liked two spirally squiggles! Well, now that my snatched body is mine to control again, allow me to introduce myself, I'm Jim "Sensei" Salicrup, the Editor-in-Chief of Papercutz, the company dedicated to publishing great graphic novels for all ages. And I welcome you to the third, trance-inducing LEGO® NINJAGO graphic novel from Papercutz.

Sharp-eyed LEGO NINJAGO fans will have noticed a couple of changes between our last LEGO NINJAGO graphic novel and this one -- the most obvious being that Cole, Zane, Jay, and Kai are in their new and improved uniforms. If you didn't notice, don't feel too bad the changes are a bit on the subtle side. The other big change this time around, is the debut of new NINJAGO artist Paul Lee. Paul is in such great demand for his incredible renderings of our favorite Masters of Spinjitzu, that he could barely fit us into his busy schedule. In fact, the artists at Space Goat and the artist from LEGO NINJAGO graphic novels #1 and 2, Paulo Henrique, all pitched in to help Mr. Lee complete this action-packed chapter in the lives of Cole, Zane, Jay, and Kai!

Fortunately, warming up in the legendary Papercutz bullpen is none other than the super-talented Jolyon Yates, whose enthusiasm and eagerness to tackle LEGO NINJAGO is inspiring! Good ol' Greg Farshtey has whipped up another spectacular script, and we're sure the results will be awesome. You will not want to miss LEGO NINJAGO graphic novel #4 "Tomb of the Fangpyre," coming soon! In the meantime, don't miss out on any Ninjago news, by logging on to www.LEGO.com as often as possible, and stay on top of all the latest news from Papercutz at www.papercutz.com. That's also where you can find out what new project Paulo Henrique is working on!

So, until next time, try to avoid staring at any sneaky snakes!

Thanks,

Jim

Geronimo Stilton

Graphic Novels Available Now: